BY KRISTA SCHADE

The Clothesline Series:

The Clothesline

Lone Wolfe – coming in 2021

Biographies:

A Living History – Uncle Col Walker

For Children:

T-Bone and the Mob, with Lisa Brettschneider

www.kristaschade.com.au

THE CLOTHESLINE

By Krista Schade

First published in 2020

Second edition published 2021

© Krista Schade 2020

A catalogue record for this work is available from the National Library of Australia

ISBN 978-0-6489020-1-0

To Kerri and Liz, Fairy's biggest fans

Krista Schade

CHAPTER 1 – THE CLOTHESLINE

My eyes flicker open and as my body awakens, I am instantly aware of the deep ache in my side, in that soft vulnerable space between my ribs and hip. I bite my lip as I ease my body over to the side of the bed, moving slowly and carefully so as not to wake him, but his arm snakes across my torso and pulls me backwards, an unwilling little spoon in a controlling embrace. He nuzzles his face into the nape of my neck and murmurs a morning greeting into my tangled bed hair. My eyes squeeze shut, unwilling to face his morning breath and empty platitudes.

He is watching the late news, the untidy pile of empty beers haphazardly strewn across the coffee table. He lashes out in protest to the latest Government updates that this lockdown will continue - the army is now enforcing residents to remain within the perimeters of their homes.

His foot connects with the coffee table leg and the beer bottles jostle together and one topples, spilling its dregs onto the wooden surface. I quickly lurch to right it, but it is too late; the drips form an accusing and expanding pool, and his face twists in rage.

The blow is not unexpected. His boot connects with my side as I am attempting to gather the bottles, and although my knees buckle and the wind rushes from my lungs I do not fall. I do not spill anything.

The morning is without incident. He is irritable but not angry and his yelling and insults are mostly aimed at the news coverage of the virus. In the kitchen the small television airs a different channel to the large screen in the lounge room and he paces back and forward between the two rooms like a caged animal, cursing world leaders and medical experts.

His mood has steadily darkened since the lockdown decision was made. His job disappeared overnight, and he is relying on the welfare payments rushed through Parliament six weeks ago when this pandemic first gripped the nation. His drinking now starts in the morning, and recently a painfully thin boy with sunken cheeks and black dead eyes has been appearing at our door every few days, delivering pills, powders, and pot. The boy accepts canned food, soft drinks and out of date bags of pasta as payment.

My days have shrunk to these few rooms, and my clothesline chats with Fairy next door. I had no job to lose, no real friends to miss and a family that he had successfully distanced over the years.

The first time he begs me to forgive him. He cries noisily and ugly, not noticing the tears and snot that mingle as he pleads with me not to go. He was sorry. He was drunk. He didn't mean it, and he loves me so much. My sister is appalled at his appearance at our parents' house and angrily yells at him to leave. She tries to shove him away from me, but I stop her. I listen to him explain and promise to change. Then I go with him to the beach for a sunset walk and when he offers his hand, I take it.

I leave him muttering into the phone to someone who shares his wild conspiracy theories around the sickness and lift a damp load of sheets from the washing machine into the plastic basket at my feet. Favouring my injured side, I carry it through the kitchen and out the back door, across the straggling lawn to the bottom of the deep yard, where the clothesline waited.

Dropping the basket on the ground I wind the clothesline up and up, until it is at its full height. I pause, one eye on the back door of the house in case he comes out, then wind it back down and start spreading the sheets across the wire lines.

It is not long before Fairy appears, having seen my clothesline signal from her own kitchen window.

I have never asked her age because although she has lived beside us since we came here four years ago, it is only recently that we have been meeting like this. I suppose she is around 60 but that might be because her waist length hair is completed grey; she moves with the agility of a younger person, but that could be because of her love of tai chi.

I had spotted her many time, early in the morning, through the splintery paling of the wooden barrier that divides our yard many times, her small hands raised as she gracefully repeated the gentle martial art movements. Until then Fairy was only someone I had nodded to on the way in or out of the house, but now I dare to think of her as a friend, but only in that very deep part of myself that is still private.

Fairy introduced herself one late afternoon when the outbreak was filling hospitals and morgues and the world seemed too surreal to be real. She was once a cook and told me about working in pubs and cafes and shearing sheds and, for a time, at a gold mine in the middle of nowhere.

Then she asked me about him. On that day, my eye was an unattractive purple and yellow shade and no amount of my depleted store of concealer could conceal. On other days she noticed a split lip, or a bruised shoulder and she asked me about them, without hesitation. I still find it astonishing that I tell Fairy everything. Perhaps it is because the world has gone crazy. Perhaps it is because that leaning fence means I can only see small slivers of her as we speak. Perhaps it is because I feel like this will end soon, one way or another.

"What are you talking to that old bag for?" His hand whips out and grabs a handful of my hair, so I am forced to face him.

"What. Did. You. Fucking. Tell. Her?" His words are low, menacing and slurred from drinking, the very worst combination. "Didja tell her I'm on the dole now? Are you talking about me to that old bag?"

My hands grip the sink which is full of cooling sudsy water and I force myself not to react, willing the gathering tears back into my soul. No cringing, no pulling away and most definitely no speaking.

He yanks my hair once more, painfully, but then lets the strands go and slinks back to the loungeroom.

"You ok today love?" Fairy speaks quietly and stays low on her side of the fence. She knows what awaits me if he sees us talking. I offer a small nod, just a slight dip of my forehead, as I continue to slowly hang the linen.

In fierce whispers we catch up, firstly on the virus, and the people we have watched carted out of homes in our streets, sometimes on stretchers, but more often in bags. The bags are the worst. They are bright yellow plastic tombs and I tell Fairy that I don't think I will ever see yellow as a happy colour again.

"Oh sweetheart," the soft voice floats over the fence. "It won't always be this bad. It'll come to an end eventually, you'll see. The news on the tele this morning said maybe as quick as six months now."

"The virus is only one nightmare," I say simply.

The dinner is savoury mince. Again. Since the lockdown I have cooked mince so many ways, but the monotony is draining for me and enraging for him, and as I hand him his plate he curses. His eyes are bloodshot – the boy has been back and there's powder on a small tray balanced frighteningly on the arm of the leather armchair.

I am not sure what happens next. More and more my mind closes off during these attacks but at the end of it I am bloodied and gasping for air. My mouth has a split that runs down both lips and I know that it will only be more painful tomorrow as the wound dries and cracks. My side has copped it again and I expect the new bruises will mingle in with the old, my very own dull rainbow. I have my hand cupped to my bleeding nose and as he clenches his raw knuckles, he looks down at me where I lie on the floor and says dismissively, "Go and have a shower." His eyes are blank, almost weary and I am proud I have not cried out.

The next day Fairy whispers fiercely to me.

"This can't go on love. He's going to kill you and he'll get away with it because the country has gone to shit!'"

Emotionless I nod and hang clothes and wince then hang some more. Today I am hanging out clean blankets that I have rewashed as an excuse to see Fairy. My home, such as it is, has never been cleaner.

Fairy looks at me worriedly noticing the near empty basket.

"You'll have to go back inside soon. Can you stay out of his way for just a bit? Maybe I can borrow a car and we might be able to get to the checkpoint and get the soldiers to help." She is a beautiful woman, my friend Fairy but I shake my head.

"No point," I say, trying not to aggravate my split lips.

Fairy reaches through the narrow crack in the fence with two wrinkled fingers and I risk quickly pressing my own to hers before I turn and slowly walk back to the house.

The next day, I stand at the sink staring aimlessly into the yard, as behind me the volume of the 24-hour news channel is raised, and more bad news spews from it. He calls for a coffee and without hesitation I fill the cup with dark liquid and deliver it to him, before returning to the sink and its familiar view.

Something next door catches my eye. A broom head appears over the fence, about halfway along the yard. It disappears then pops back up again, repeating the action every few seconds. It is so comical that I simply watch for several moments before it clicks. Fairy's clothesline is older than mine, so it is rusted in place, but perhaps she is signalling me with the broom. I walk to the laundry for a basket and, forcing myself to move slowly and quietly, I venture outside.

Fairy is waiting for me.

"Here," she hisses and with one brief toss lobs a small glass jar over to me. I quickly grab it from where it lands and toss it into the basket.

"What is it?" The jar contains some sort of clear liquid, but there are foamy bubbles sloshing atop the fluid, which seems viscous and slimy.

"Danny Davis from number 43 hasn't got long to go. They'll probably bag him tonight or tomorrow." Her voice is low, and the words fall rapidly from her. I think she is saying the uncaring words quickly, to ease the sting of them.

"That's his spit. Well, saliva," she corrects. "And it will be full of the virus." Our eyes meet through a crack in the fence.

"How did you get it?" I ask, feeling the panic rise in my chest. The jar nestles in the folds of towels and still has the label attached, strawberry jam. It seems ridiculous that something so deadly is so casually contained by a jar that once held a sugary breakfast spread.

"I went and got it. Danny knows what he's like and as he faces his maker he wants to help." Fairy is almost abrupt now. "Put it in his food – today – while it's still fresh." Her eyes meet mine again. "This has to end."

The jar feels like it is burning my hand as I gingerly carry it into the kitchen. The news is still blaring but he has passed out on the couch. For a moment I pause wondering if I can go through with this, but my survival instinct kicks in and in moments I have prepared two sandwiches, a large glass of cordial and even a piece of cake, all laced with Danny's gift. I deliver the food to the lounge room and try not to watch as he gulps down the drink before working through the sandwiches and cake.

When he finishes eating, he lets out an appreciative burp, offers uncharacteristic thanks and fires up the water pipe, filling his lungs and the house with the pungent smell of scorched marijuana. I take the plates and glass back to the kitchen and plunge them into the boiling soapy water I had scrubbed my hands in earlier.

The rest of the day passes. The boy visited earlier in the week but is back today and from the look of him he may not be around much longer. He is visibly sweating, and his cough is deep and hacking, the gasps rattling his whole thin and pale body. The men in suits that constantly star on television say this virus is moving faster than ever and looking at the boy I tend to believe them; he seemed fine a couple of days ago.

He makes the boy throw the package into our house and in return tosses him a packet of chocolate biscuits and a can of lemonade. It seems the economy is rapidly descending to the 'beggars can't be choosers' premise. He kicks the plastic bag package across the shabby lounge room carpet to me and tells me to wash it all off.

"But don't get anything wet," he yells over his shoulder. "And be careful," he adds. I am an afterthought.

For the first time in a long time fate is on my side. The boy's supply seemed to change without reason, and I had learned to dread the ones with powder, because his rage and mania went through the roof. This package contains some dried green leaf encased in foil, and a mishmash of pharmaceuticals, all unboxed and no two blister packs the same. There are 18 packs in total, some with tabs missing, leaving random spaces like broken teeth, where the long-gone true owner had once popped the medication free. I grab my phone and quickly punch in the various brand names emblazoned on the back of the blister packs. One search delivers incredibly good news. Lorazepam. A muscle relaxant. I cannot believe my luck.

Once wiped down with disinfectant I stuff the useful blister packs into my bra and take the remaining cards of pills and metallic bag of pot back into him. He snaps one pill out of the pack and dry swallows it, before reaching for the water pipe again and reclines in the creaking armchair, browsing channels idly between inhales. Believing he has no further instructions for me I turn to leave but he reaches out and cruelly squeezes my breast, scoffing at the way my face displays the pain I feel as the tender flesh protests. Without a word he drops his hand and I rush to the kitchen, one breast is burning but the other, untouched, still hides a deadly secret.

Later in the day he finally falls asleep and from then on, I am in charge. I add crushed pills to each drink and as he starts to burn with a fever, I use rubber gloves and an old tee shirt as a facemask whenever I venture into the loungeroom. He looks at me confusedly that second day but as the virus and pills combine, he is soon a puddle of a man, bathed in sweat and his own urine, unable to leave the place he once cruelly ruled.

No longer under threat I mostly sit in the kitchen, towels and plastic shower curtains forming a protective barrier around the loungeroom doorways, and when his coughing becomes laboured and loud, I raise the volume of the small kitchen television.

I cannot say if it is the progress of the virus or the poisons I have delivered, but on the evening of the fifth day the coughing and gasping stops, and in the quiet and calm house I carry a change of clothes into the bathroom and take a long, hot cleansing shower. I wash my hair, shave my legs, and use floral scented scrub on my face. I dry my hair with hot blasts from the dryer, pull on fresh clothes and walk down the back steps and out into the yard.

I find the loosest boards and wrestle them away from the fence, until I create a space large enough to slip through to the neighbouring garden. As I walk towards the house, Fairy appears and holds open the door. Her relief is evident in her gasp of joy and she welcomes me inside with love and kindness beaming across her face.

"Hello love. I've been waiting for you."

Then my tears come.

CHAPTER 2 – FAIRY

Fairy was used to being alone. It was not something she had chosen for herself, but it seemed it was what the universe unilaterally decided for her. As the only daughter of uncomplicated, hard-working parents she silently witnessed the agony of miscarriages and stillbirths that wore down her parents with grief, until they simply gave up ever adding to their family.

The trio moved around dusty inland country, taking work where it was offered, living in a series of outhouses and workers cottages before settling in a small town on the highway. The narrow strip of bitumen shimmered in the hot dry summers and washed out when the rains came, but it provided a shaky conduit to the outside world.

As a child on the cusp of womanhood, balancing on a tightrope of conflicting hormones, the stretch of road delivered excitement to Fairy atop Greyhound buses, long road trains and family station wagons with steaming overheated radiators. Their home was a small cottage and as her parents both headed to work in the town it was left to Fairy to amuse herself from morning to night, and she spent hours hung over the front fence, amongst the wild passionfruit vine, watching the world traipse by.

As the years passed without change to upset the family's monotony, Fairy grew into a woman. Her wispy blonde hair reached her waist and her face and slim limbs tanned in the harsh outback sun. Her father joked that although her hair grew, her legs did not, and her slight stature earned her the nickname that she embraced.

Schooling came and went, also without neither triumph nor failure. With much more emphasis on earning a living, Fairy left her parents, travelled along the beckoning highway to a vast homestead that sat squatly on wide green plains, many hours away. She learned quickly, mimicking the movements of the experienced station cook, watching and mirroring the way dough was pulled and stretched, and the way meat was stripped from bones before hitting an angrily spitting pan.

Cooking came naturally to Fairy and she worked from dawn till dusk, preparing meals for the hungry men that toiled across the station, not eating herself until the lunch packs for the next day were wrapped in paper and cloth, and stored in sturdy metal pails. The station cook grew wary of Fairy's talents and deftly shipped her off to the shearing shed to live and work among the contractors that visited twice each year to remove the prized fleeces.

It was here, in a kitchen built of timber and cast iron, bothered by the flies and heat, that Fairy fell in love. He was a roustabout, and his job was to quickly sweep up the wool behind the shearers and move it away to the classing table. The shearers gave him a hard time, tripping him up and smearing the handle of his broom with grease, but Fairy thought he was the most beautiful man she had ever seen.

At 19, a full two years older than herself, he was tall and strong with a head-full of wild brown curls that flopped over his eyes when he looked in her direction. They snatched moments alone together, to talk and smile shyly at each other, in an innocent way that seemed so childlike and sweet whenever Fairy travelled back in time to remember him. Without much prompting she can effortlessly recall the delicious flutter she felt in her stomach whenever their eyes met; a simple glance filled her with a warmth that made her days worthwhile.

Shearing came to a natural end, and she shared one passionate, desperate kiss with the boy as they closed the shed and packed up the kitchen, before he was gone. Despite his feverishly whispered assurances he did not appear when the team returned six months later.

The boss simply shrugged when Fairy asked where he was, and that was that - despite the leaden weight in her heart and hidden tears in the dark, she never saw that beautiful boy again.

Karma cruelly intervened whenever happiness fluttered its joyous vibrations in Fairy's direction. She endured lost loves, kind friends who turned vicious and betrayed her, and the gut-wrenching agony of holding a tiny pale lifeless body in her hands. The burning ache between her legs that hot day was unmatched by the sorrow that wept in her hardening heart.

As the years marched forward and time cycled past Fairy withdrew more and more. She moved across two states following work and her whim, as if blown by an unseen zephyr of hot breath. Her parents passed much as they lived, quietly and without fuss, until only she was left of their family.

She was kind and gentle, showing gracious compassion to everyone who crossed her path but taking care, always, not to become known, or to know another. She cooked more meals than she had any hope of remembering, and with every steaming plate offered a friendly yet routine greeting, and her smile rarely reached her eyes, until one day she found herself retired on a small pension, in a quiet suburb on the outskirts of the city.

For fifteen years she lived undisturbed, the community large enough to suit her craving for anonymity, yet the traffic was slow, and the streets lined with towering trees.

When the young couple moved in next door Fairy offered a neighbourly nod and occasional hello if their paths crossed but, if she was being frank - as was her nature - she was relieved when they seemed uninterested in anything more. He struck her as brash; stocky with an abrupt cold-hearted way of speaking, while she was always noticeably quiet and nervous, but they took up little of Fairy's interest.

Unlike Danny Davis at number 43. Newly widowed, his arrival at the cottage on the other side of Fairy's modest home was heralded by a noisy gang of his adult children and a mob of scampering laughing grandchildren. She had heard the truck as it pulled up on the street on moving day, some six or seven years ago now, because the brakes released a screech that set off the Great Dane across the road. Several cars arrived and parked, and a chattering human chain proceeded to disgorge what seemed like a lifetime of treasures out of the truck and into the house.

Danny disrupted everything Fairy had carefully crafted for herself. He persisted, determined to form a friendship - nothing more, mind you - plying her with baked treats, vegetables from his garden and taking her bin to the kerb when it rained on garbage day. She politely maintained her distance, physically and emotionally, for a long time, but his cheerful insistence that they be mates eventually wore her down. Against her better judgement Danny worked his way into her small, ordered life. For many years now they have shared sunny front porch beers, exchanged small Christmas gifts, and generally enjoying each other's company. It was a beautifully platonic friendship that defied Fairy's bad luck.

Until now.

Fairy sighs as she strips off the plastic shoe covers and steps onto the strip of lawn in her back garden, before stooping to untie her shoes. It was not easy, given she was still wearing the rubber washing up gloves. Once her feet are released from the leather trainers, she drops them, the gloves and shoe covers into a bucket of bleach, before removing her apron and face mask. These too she drops into the bucket, followed by the plastic shower cap that releases waves of grey hair as she listlessly pulls it from her head. She submerges the lot under the water and covers the bucket with a lid, which she removes from a second plastic tub, sitting nearby. From that she withdraws yesterday's shoes, cap, mask, apron and gloves and quickly hangs them on the small clothes horse, erected on the concrete path.

Her remaining clothes she wears into the shower, where she lathers up with precious store-bought soap, now so eagerly sought after, before finally she can strip off and scrub her bare skin. Eventually she emerges, hangs the dripping outfit in the spare room to dry, before reaching for the bottle of whiskey that sits in the centre of her kitchen table. These days she needs a strong drink after visiting Danny. She needs the burning liquid to remind her she is still alive, and to help chase the tears away.

She knows he will be gone soon, and her tired mind shies away from thinking about that day. She is in full self-protection mode; has been since the virus hit. She no longer watches much news, preferring re-runs of sitcoms and inane reality shows, but sometimes the ticker tape of pandemic updates intrudes even the lightest entertainment. She listens to playlists of show tunes and songs from the 70s, singing along to lyrics full of love and hope, even as she keeps an eye on the top of the clothesline over the fence.

Unless she ventures out for food, Fairy's world had shrunk two these two neighbours. Danny, with his ever-present sheen of sweat and ghostly grey eyes, and Tasmin, the bruised and forlorn child bride, who she grew more and more concerned for, with each passing day. From her seat in the front window Fairy notes how many times the young drug mule visits and listens with a heavy heart to the thuds and crashes that too often follow soon after. She hears him rage and thunder, but it had been a long time since she had heard Tasmin's voice at a regular pitch - their conversations were now held in furtive whispers between the palings.

It takes another two shots of whiskey before the sleeping pill began to work and Fairy gratefully falls into a deep sleep, filled with anxious, dark dreams she refuses to remember the next day.

"It's getting worse, Dan." She paces across the deep pile carpet that spreads across her neighbour's bedroom, her plastic shoe covers creating crackling static electricity with every stride.

"She's black and blue today. Can hardly move. He's so far from reality he's dangerous. I have to do something." It was not really a question, and Danny's short chuckle bought on another painful bout of coughing. Fairy suddenly stops pacing and hands him the child's sippy cup of juice, trying to help him raise it, but hampered by the damn rubber gloves.

Her friend sips gratefully but with little energy. He's so weak, Fairy thinks. How could it only be a week ago that they spoke casually from one porch to the next, only days since the virus had forced him to his bed?

"It's the drugs," Danny's voice is rasping, his throat horse from the hacking cough that plagues him and the fever that seems to be dehydrating him where he lay.

"Bullshit," Fairy snaps, uncharacteristically harsh. She has not spoken to Dan like that since the first time he tried to say hello across the back fence, all those years ago. If memory serves her correctly, at the time she had told him to bugger off and mind his own business. The recollection brings a sad smile to her heart and when she meets his eye now, she sees a brief glimmer of the old Danny in his tepid grin, that tells her he too is remembering.

With a sigh she sits on the plastic stool at the end of the bed.

"Sorry." She rubs both hands - gloves - up and down her cheeks as if to wipe away everything that is happening around her.

"This *thing* has made everything mad, but I think he," she jerks her head in the direction of Tasmin's house, "was mad beforehand. He was *bad* before all this." Danny does not disagree; he is already asleep again, his chest heaving up and down as his infection laden breath rattles in and out.

The next day when Fairy visits Danny he is waiting for her and seems brighter somehow, more alert. She eyes him cautiously but listens without interrupting when he speaks. She remains patient as he struggles to reveal his plan in its simplistic entirety. It is risky; if Tasmin is caught Fairy doubts she will survive, but as instructed she finds a small glass jar and holds it close as Daniel coughs and coughs. For an hour she sits with him, neither speaking, as they harvest the vile liquid from deep within his diseased lungs.

As she readies to leave, she prepares another tray for Daniel, and on it places some juice and water in toddler cups covered in garish designs, a bowl of honey and a spoon to soothe his raw throat and a new stock of tissues. As she turns to leave Danny quietly speaks, "Thank you. And goodbye. Please don't come back tomorrow Fairy."

Her eyes burn with hot stinging tears as she rips off the protective layer and flees into her home. As the water runs over her body Fairy collapses to the bottom of her shower and sobs and screams and rages until she is exhausted.

It takes some time before she is composed enough to re-dress and when she wanders listlessly back to the quiet kitchen, she is almost surprised to find the small jar sitting innocently on the table. In her grief and rage she does not remember even carrying back through the fence, but here it sits, Danny's gift.

Pacing up and down alongside her fence holding her broom above her head strikes Fairy as utterly ridiculous but, in these times, what even *was* normal?

She begins to giggle at the spectacle she must present, but her chuckles are somewhat manic, and she struggles for composure as Tasmin appears at the clothesline. In rapid feverish whispers Fairy explains to her Danny's plan, and with one swift movement she lobs the jar over the fence where it lands on the struggling lawn. For a brief and agonising moment Fairy fears she will not take it, but through the gap in the fence sees it disappear to hide into the basket of washing.

There is nothing more to do but wait. Fairy keeps an eye on the clothesline, but it does not move, and she hopes it is a good sign, but is fearful of that hope. Without Daniel to look in on and needing to keep busy, she tidies her home, restlessly moving through the rooms dusting, organising, and rearranging. She pulls everything from the spare room and returns it to a guest suite, complete with fresh flowers she changes each day.

On Wednesday - or is it Thursday? - there is a tap at her back door and there stands Tasmin, looking calm but tired, with faded yellow bruises still visible on her chin and one cheekbone. As she welcomes her up the back step and into the kitchen, Fairy is momentarily distracted by the rush of uncomplicated joy of realisation and optimism, that floods her body and makes her limbs feel light.

With Tasmin to fuss over she does not glance out the front window so does not see the van pull up at number 43. She does not see the figure in a frightening white hazmat suit, guide a steel trolley on unco-operative wheels up the uneven path. She does not have to witness the figure, carrying yellow plastic, enter Danny's home.

CHAPTER 3 – DANNY'S GIFT

When Laura Davis received the phone call from the medical centre, all those years ago, she made an appointment to see the specialist the next day, with her trademark efficiency. She calmly repeated the date and time to the understanding receptionist, and neatly wrote the details in her small pocket diary as well as on the Guide Dogs calendar on the fridge. *Tuesday 16th, 2.45pm, Market Street Surgery.*

She told Danny about the call when he wandered into the kitchen that evening, having spent the afternoon helping their eldest son at the renovator's delight he had recently purchased, not too far from their own home. *Renovator's nightmare* was how Laura described it, but only to herself. She would never upset any of the kids and in this economy, it was all anyone could afford when they were starting out, unless they wanted to be right out in the suburbs. *Perish the thought.*

Danny immediately pushed for more details.

"What did the doctor say, exactly? Tell me what she said exactly." Laura explained she had not spoken to the doctor yet.

"Then what did the bloody reception girl say?" he demanded, his worry presenting as irritability. Laura patiently explained that the bloody receptionist was actually a very experienced practice nurse, and Danny shouldn't make sexist assumptions and that their conversation was brief and would he please stop stomping around the kitchen.

The exasperation in her voice made him quit pacing instantly and instead he had gathered her into his arms for a hug, and kissed the top of her head, right in the centre where those few stubborn greys defied her every effort.

When Danny thinks back to that day now it is all a blur. He knows he went with his wife to the appointment and can remember her pointed look when a very officious middle-aged practice nurse kindly ushered them to the waiting area. *Experienced medical professional, you dickhead,* her raised eyebrow told him. If he quietens his mind, even now he can remember back to how calm and serene Laura seemed, but the desperately tight grip she had on his hand as they sat across from the oncologist told him all he needed to know.

He does not know now what the doctor said that day. Oh, he knows that he took it all in at the time, those dreadful details about treatment and medication and experimental techniques, but as time passed those mundane and useless details have been washed away. It seems to Danny that every bout of sobbing, every time he railed against the unfairness of losing her, every snot-filled and futile tantrum wiped out everything but the most precious of memories.

As he closes his eyes now, he can remember meeting her, a friend of a friend watching the cricket in a group of people he no longer recalls, bathed in sunshine and shyly talking to him - him! He remembers how stressful it was to organise their wedding, on a shoestring budget but with so many people they wanted to include; all that stress had disappeared when he saw her at the other end of the narrow church aisle. He remembers the joy they shared with each pregnancy and birth and how his heart ached as he sat with her through the despair of losing her parents.

The way she raised their boys could not be forgotten by him or any of their four sons, that beautiful, uniquely Laura combination of adoration and frank humour. She wasn't blind to the boisterous and often downright naughty behaviour of their children, but she managed them all with poise and a confident grace. Until recently their every conversation since Laura's death had been peppered with what they called "mum-isms" or tales of how she steadfastly defended her family, right to the end. At her funeral each of the boys and their wives spoke freely of basking in her unconditional love, and Danny thought that was exactly the right way to describe his Laura - unconditional.

With her gone he grew to hate their once beloved home, even though it was where her garden grew, and her furniture stood; without her it was simply empty. It felt cold despite central heating and dark despite large sun filled rooms. It was full of memories that brought joy and heartbreak in equal measure, and the gardens did not want to respond to him the way the plants had blossomed under Lara's touch. It did not take much thought to come to the decision. He cashed in the house in a newly trendy location and bought a small war era cottage out on the outskirts of the city, making a tidy profit in the process. The money meant he could live comfortably in retirement, even after sharing some with delighted grandchildren, and despite the family protests, he held fast and moved into number 43.

The slower pace and greater sense of community suited him, and he quickly made many friends; the young couple across the road with the big dogs, the Indian family who shared the most incredibly sensual curries with him and the special needs kids who lived together in a group home on the corner. He shared vegetables from his small plot, having decided to give flowers the flick in favour of fruit and other delicacies, and he kept the path clear for young children on pushbikes to whizz safely by. He found a good butcher, he enjoyed the senior's discount beers and gigantic schnitzels at the local club, and he cheerfully hung sporadically blinking Christmas lights from his veranda each December.

Getting to know Fairy was a lot harder. To begin with, her snubs did not faze him much but as time went on, he began to see it as a personal challenge to crack her tough exterior. The kids received updates of his efforts when he chatted over the phone or they made the noisy trek out to see him on weekends. Danny had hoped the sounds of kids squealing and laughing in the backyard would draw her out, but it seemed to push her even further away. Instead, after many unsuccessful attempts, he decided to change tack and began leaving vegetables at her door; plump sun-ripened tomatoes, creamy white cauliflowers nestled in thick green leaves and bunches of pungent basil. To begin with she was blatant in her efforts to ignore his attempts at friendship but eventually, over glasses of various tipples shared on one or the other of their front porches, they fell into an uncomplicated understanding of each other's needs. Danny needed company and to be liked, while Fairy needed a mate, despite her protests, but could not care less whether she was admired.

Dan sighs and shuffles in the wide bed, the sheets clammy and damp with perspiration, and tries to make his aching body comfortable. He misses the boys with every raw fibre of his soul. At the beginning of the lockdown, they regularly spoke as a family, staying connected by video call and phone but as the months passed and the pandemic threw the world into a frenzied chaos the internet connection became less and less reliable.

Visits in person were outlawed and the streets patrolled by the military, until the vast reach of the virus kept everyone home regardless, terrified and helpless. Daniel was not there when his grandson was laid to rest and offering comfort to his distraught parents via a sketchy phone connection was obscene and cruel and broke his heart apart all over again.

Dan knew how he had contracted the virus - community transmission the medicos called it. Despite following all the guidelines and only venturing outside his home for groceries once the home deliveries stopped, the inevitable had happened anyway. Contaminated droplets had entered his old man's body, and rapidly moved through every cell, dragging them all down into the black toxic sludge that now invades his nightmares.

After six months of the illness – a global pandemic, the news called it - even the most basic of retail services had all but disappeared. Home deliveries ended, as workers refused to risk their own health and now everyone was subjected to a complicated system of grocery store visits by roster, depending on your address. Number 43 meant Daniel could shop every three weeks, on a Wednesday, and he had been provided a list of outlets allocated to his address. The process was time consuming, involving emergency service workers checking everyone's identification and cross-matching details against the rosters on small portable devices, held in gloved hands. There were limits on how much he could buy, how long he could be in one store and where he must stand to line up. He understood the need, but the red tape had proven almost as suffocating as the illness.

To visit the shops Daniel donned old sneakers, that he now kept hanging on a hook on the veranda post. He covered his clothes with rubber fishing waders and a tatty plastic coat, that Laura had insisted he kept in the boot of their car. It was useless to leave it there now - the car had not moved for months - so it became part of his outdoors protection. Over his face went one of those flip down face shields that he had been able to score from the lovely Indian fellow from down the road - when his wife and children all passed, he sorrowfully found himself with too many masks and gave a grateful Dan one of the spares. Over thinning hands he snapped a pair of disposable gloves, the one item he refused to reuse, and the one thing he had a seemingly unending supply of. While not exactly a hoarder Laura had kept their former home well stocked, with all sorts of stores, for any occasion, and somehow the six cartons of latex gloves had made their way from the old house to the new. Small blessings, he had mused, when he uncovered them anew, from their home at the bottom of the laundry cupboard.

After that moment on the lawn - that moment that changed everything but was a mere six days ago - he had locked his doors and tacked a note in a pale blue envelope onto the back door. This is how he and Fairy visited during the lockdown, slinking though the dividing fence and using the entrances at the rear of their homes, to avoid fines for breaking social distancing rules. He remembered hearing her rattle the locked door, then the pause as she read the letter he had written. He knew she was stubborn - oh how he knew it! - but he had prayed and hoped she would stay away. He needed to protect the last person he cared for, the last person he had been able to share this desperate, horrendous time with, but he knew he could only wait and hope. Wait and hope for Fairy to heed his wishes, and for symptoms to somehow pass him by.

The letter was brief and in it, in his messy handwriting that had always irritated Laura, Dan explained how he had seen the wretched drug mule stumble and collapse on his front lawn. He had opened the front door and called out to the boy, who was conscious and weakly attempting to stand. Dan wrote to Fairy that he had tentatively gone outside, with a carton of milk and half eaten box of cereal, hoping to at least fill the lad's belly on what must surely be his final day. He had kept his distance, knowing full well how far the virus could carry once airborne, but when the boy croaked a grateful thanks

Danny had leaned forward to gently pat his shoulder in sympathy.

It was then the coughing started and instantly Dan knew his mistake.

He does not write in the letter how he immediately retreated inside without a further thought to the boy, a memory that makes him burn in shame, a deep-seated burn that heats him more than any fever could. He had immediately scrubbed himself raw in a scalding shower, gargled with mouthwash and forced himself to vomit into the drain as the water fell around him, but in his soul he feared the worst.

It was hours before the panic in his chest subsided enough for him to consider the boy, but when Dan peeked through the slatted blinds to the front lawn, it was empty in the pre-dusk light. Ultimately neither of them would see each other again; up close or from afar. From that moment Daniel kept all blinds and curtains drawn, keeping the world out in an empty attempt to stave off the chemical reactions already taking place within his body.

What he did write in the note to his neighbour was that he had decided to stay locked in for two or three weeks until he saw what illness, if any, developed and that Fairy must stay away until then. The fever started the next day, all too quickly followed by the hacking cough and thick lung congestion, and by that evening Fairy had broken the pane in the kitchen door and visited him like a plastic encased Florence Nightingale.

He is not too proud to be grateful. Her visits bring him a meagre supply of medicine and company he needs to keep him sane as he faces the inevitable. Her concerns for the bullied and bruised lass at number 39 were growing and it was not a leap for Danny to offer a solution. When he suggests the plan, he already knows how quickly the virus is making its way through his cells; he can feel the drawing down of his health. He sees in the flash of horror across Fairy's face, but he also notes how quickly that feeling of abhorrence was replaced with an emotion Fairy could only describe to him as an uneasy optimism. As they discuss the plan, she in rapid, almost excitable spurts and he in laboured words of logic, they agree Tasmin had little hope of surviving without their help, and it is settled.

Tonight, as he lies against the dank, stale pillows making final preparations he marvels at how much has changed. His beloved Laura is gone, his family isolated in their own tiny pieces of the city, and his own morals are now so incredibly warped he has set up a murder with little hesitation or guilt. The world has changed so much that he believes another death will hardly even matter and if his sin creates a better life for young Tasmin, and Fairy, he will explain his reasoning at the gates of heaven later tonight.

His fever addled mind is not certain what he will seek forgiveness for first; abetting in the murder of another or for taking his own life, such as it is. He swallows the last of Laura's strong pain medication, one small, bitter powerful pill after another, and as they dissolve, he welcomes the warm fuzziness that suffuses his sore bones and eases his aching heavy chest. He closes his eyes and allows his breath to slow, as the drugs and virus combine to stop the beating of his broken heart.

CHAPTER 4 – THE DRIVER

Dale steers the van to a stop at the kerb, more from habit than from need. The streets are so empty he could have parked in the centre of the road with ease; in fact, he could leave the van just about anywhere these days without any need to jostle for position. The entire city is eerily quiet, which made his gruesome task all the ghastlier, but by now his nervous system is so overloaded with grief and terror he barely feels anything.

He had never been one to take his job for granted nor had he ever been anything other than cheerful and polite. Dale was the kind of guy who whistled as he worked, and in a previous life, less than half a year ago, he had happily toiled for long hours alongside the other Council workers. He worked in the city's various parks and public gardens, a profession he quietly adored. He was not highly paid, but he was highly skilled and had a knack for coaxing tired plants into flourishing jungles of verdant green. He had relished working outdoors and enjoyed the camaraderie of his teammates, a jangle of nationalities and ages, genders and personalities who - most of the time - happily got along and kept the city looking spruce.

The parkies ignored the office politics and had no interest in being part of the who's who; some staff thrived on the drama and ladder climbing, but Dale's bunch was immune to the histrionics that plagued the office bound city Council staff.

When the pandemic first hit, it quietly and sneakily snaked its way into the country via airports and cruise ships, meaning their beachside, holiday destination city was one of the first to feel the effects. Infected tourists and corporate types who did not even feel unwell yet, disgorged from crowded planes and trains or came ashore with just a small cough, to spread the unseen contagion like a dirty secret.

As panic set in and Governments across the world scrambled to contain the uncontainable, teams of Council workers were re-allocated to pandemic control assignments. Dale first worked to set up solid concrete barricades and heavy padlocked chains to close off his beloved parks, then joined the units responsible for disinfecting the streets. His horticultural knowledge was used to calculate how to best cover the roads and pavements with a dwindling supply of disinfecting chemicals, and when the precious liquid was used up, he and his team used their heavy equipment to dig graves in the once pristine lawns of the city parks.

He has done this for months, excavating wide tranches that rip apart the swathes of green grass like wounds. With every hour spent tearing apart the earth, Dale can feel his gentle heart wither and dry into something unrecognisable, like a leaf ripped from the branch.

Sometimes, to their horror, they are tasked with creating new trenches right beside where other moon suit clad staff unload bodies into mass graves beside them. Sometimes Dale spends an entire shift, looking forward, not daring to allow his gaze to slide sideward.

The Council and other emergency services, joined by some hardy volunteers, now work alongside the military, a band of weary shell-shocked Brothers or Sisters at Arms. They work on a roster; sometimes they collect bodies from homes and hospitals and wherever else the infected fell, sometimes burying the dead and sometimes working on the construction of a large crematorium the sombre experts said will soon be needed.

The rosters vary without pattern as names suddenly appear, or more dreadfully, disappear, from the lists of work gangs.

Dale's family live more than a day away, across the mountains and far from the coast, in a small inland town on the highway. He believes his parent's and both sister's families were safe, but communication was such a problem that he had not been able to contact them for three weeks now. Resources were stretched so thinly across this huge country that internet and phone services had been withdrawn from a lot of places, in favour of providing a more stable connection for official use.

The last he had heard was that the infections in his hometown were still low, and those who showed any symptoms were being quarantined at the small local hospital. His dad told him that the bridge was now barricaded, and no entry across the river was permitted; a hometown militia was in control, under the auspices of Bob the Police Sergeant. It did not sound exactly legal but both he and his father agree it is absolutely necessary. When he told his father about the deaths in the city it seemed too unreal to be true, but he needed them to know how serious it was here, so they kept safe. He needed them to be safe.

He fears he has left it too late for his own children, and that knowledge drives him beyond the point of despair. He barely sleeps and days off are not possible, yet he continues to work without complaint, desperate to contain this epidemic before it reaches his girls.

When the infection rate in the city had skyrocketed in a matter of days, he and Kate had discussed sending their daughters to his parents, but they dithered; it was too far, they both had to work, surely it'd be fine. The realisation the effect their inaction could have, is a dragging, leaden weight in the pit of Dale's stomach. They left it too late to leave or to have the girls shipped out and now they were in a dangerous dance to keep them safe.

It did not help to know many of his co-workers were in a similar situation; some had already lost wives, parents, neighbours and, most tragically, too many children. When the virus swept across the world, the news reports seemed too unbelievable to be true and the shaky, leaked video footage added a macabre Hollywood effect to the story. They had all been taken by surprise. Tricked by their complacency, and completely unable to fathom this new reality that lay just ahead. Dale knew he and Kate had been lucky - so far - but that knowledge was no comfort to him at all. The fact he did not - could not - feel lucky, and could no longer count on his good fortune, caused Dale painful stabs of guilt, and a further piece of his mind quietly fractures with each realisation.

This week Dale is on collections. It sounds innocent enough, but it is not. At the start of all this they had worked in pairs, but now collections means seven days of working alone, with a list of addresses, a supply of body bags and a former delivery van that fills so quickly.

Dale does not know where the addresses come from. He assumes family members contact the hotline, or perhaps neighbours reported a body in a garden or on a street. He suspects some people call in for themselves, knowing by the time they arrived it would be past their end. He does not know, does not *want* to know, the classified details, but in the past few months Dale has had the misfortune to collect ravaged bodies from almost every street in this part of the city.

The work is never ending. The list is live, meaning the dreadful inventory on his tablet device is continually updated as new information is provided to hotline operators. After each collection he presses 'refresh' and filters his catalogue to the postcode in which he is allocated, before moving to the next house. It feels like the worst kind of Groundhog Day imaginable.

In a full hazmat suit that keeps his nervous sweat trapped stickily inside it, he enters the home via the unlocked front door and efficiently locates the main bedroom. His mind reminds him how similar the layout of homes is, now that he had seen inside so many. He allows his imagination to wander freely - anything to distract him from the reality of the actions he is undertaking. As he zippers the bag over the man's grey, sunken face he counts off the floor plan types; there were the two front bedroom type houses, like this one, the walk straight into the loungeroom homes and those that he now called backwards, where the front entry led into the kitchen and the rest of the house opened onto back yards. He thinks about all the collectors in all the suburbs in all the countries and wonders if they are budding architects too, but the sheer numbers involved is something his mind quickly retreats away from.

Stretchers are no longer used to remove patients (*bodies*) from their homes. The new solo collection process involves strapping the body onto a removalist trolley, because it can be done almost single-handedly, depending on the size of the deceased.

This man was tall but slim and the virus had swept all weight from him, so Dale is able to gently manoeuvre him without incident. After he affixes a barcode to the bag and scans it with the tablet, he removes the empty bottle of pills from the bedside table; he would toss it out the window of the van later, and at least save the family any further questions.

If there is any family left, Dale thinks. The information given to him lists the man in the crackling yellow bag as the sole occupant, so as he leaves Dale locks the front door and tacks up an official warning notice to its wooden face. The latest advice claims the virus remains active for a fair while on surfaces, so hopefully everyone keeps away.

Three times today he fills a van and returns it to the processing centre at what was once his Council depot. Each time he adjusts the information in the tablet, steps out of the van filled with yellow bags and into an empty one, waiting in the car park. He speaks to very few people, and he chooses never to look back. There were many people and officials milling around, each with a vital job to do in this terrible process, but the crowd barely speaks. There is no chatting, no smiling, nothing but numb robotic progress and a harrowing set of tasks that he fears he will not ever recover from.

If I survive, a small voice reminds him.

Dale is considered HIGH RISK due to the ongoing exposure to the bodies of those he transported and the work he does at the mass graves now that the airborne threat has been confirmed by scientists. There had been talk of housing high risk workers in barracks style accommodation, but all the boarding schools, community halls and barracks are being used to try to treat the sick, so once his shift was over and he has been decontaminated Dale walks the 30 minutes back to his home. As an essential worker he is permitted to use his car, or even the trail bike he used to enjoy riding on weekends, and he is eligible for a fuel allowance from the Government, but he finds he needs those 30 minutes twice each day, for himself.

When he leaves in the morning, he uses the walk to prepare himself for what lies ahead, to fortify his mind and hang onto what is left of his sanity. Each evening he spends the time to separate the horror behind him from the joy that lies ahead, even if he could only enjoy it at arm's length.

The home he and Kate bought when they were first married is eerily familiar to the loungeroom-at-the-front homes he visits when collecting. Fortunately for him, it also boasts a side door on the western edge of the house, that leads into the laundry and main bathroom. This is now where Dale lives. He sleeps on a single camp cot, and his clothes and belongings replacing the usual cleaning assortments that the cupboards once held.

Kate and the girls sleep in what was once the bedroom he shared with his wife and use the smaller en suite bathroom and rest of the house. Dale sleeps each night with his phone crooning an easy listening playlist, to stave off the quiet loneliness.

Over the months, the sliver of anger festered between him and Kate when they realised the danger they were all in, and became a solid wedge of resentment as Dale's job put them all at risk. He had nowhere else to go, and the clear plastic shower curtain that he secured between the laundry and the rest of their home, allowed him the only contact he had with his daughters. To begin with Kate had asked him to keep the door locked.

Taylor is their inquisitive toddler, who happily babbles to him about her day through the barrier, but Dale aches to hold her in his arms and breathe in the smell of her. He struggles each evening to keep her attention; the sorrow he feels in his fragile heart when she distractedly skips away out of sight fills him with anguish.

Bridie is only a baby, just learning to crawl and pull herself up onto furniture, and this meant Kate had been forced to barricade the doorway with a side table. Bridie often eyed him through the gently swaying curtain like he was some sort of exotic pet.

She doesn't know who I am. Dale does not know how this can ever work out well. There were too many gaps in their lives. Too many unrepairable fractures. Too many moments lost.

The vast distance between Dale and Kate yawns open like a canyon, and it hangs in the air of their home like a bitter fog. Their conversation is all admin.

"How many?"

"Three van loads."

"There was no bread, so I've made some and it's pretty bad."

"Mike isn't well; he's been sent home."

"Taylor swore today. On the phone. To my mother. Don't smile, it wasn't funny."

"The riots were bad again today. No one is being arrested though."

"The tap near the vegies was dripping again, but I think I've fixed it."

I love you Kate, please remember that. Remember us. That remains unsaid.

CHAPTER 5 – KATE'S CHOICE

Kate does not notice the tired sigh that quietly escapes her bright red lips as she stops at the makeshift sanitation station in the foyer of the building, but the sound does not go unnoticed.

"Tired love?" The security guard's expression behind his rigid plastic face shield shone with kind concern, and Kate feels a shameful guilt at his sympathy.

She shakes her head at him and rolls her eyes a little, attempting to inject a lightness she did not feel into her reply. With a nod of her head she indicates the row of staff, evenly spaced along the reception room, each engrossed in wiping down their bags, shoes, phones, and lunch boxes before they entered the Parliament.

"I'm just sick of all this." Ironically, she speaks the half-truth with honesty, even if it was not the direct cause of her sigh, and reaches for her own alcohol wipes and disinfectant, as her temperature is taken, and her throat swabbed. In reality, it is her self-reproach that exhausts her.

Since the outbreak, the Government has protected the inner sanctity of the Parliament building with fervour, ordering a level of hygienics destined to defy the deadly virus, known as VS-202, after the scientist and laboratory who identified it. If all whimsey and joy had not disappeared from the world, Kate would have found it humorous that someone wished for fame so badly they willingly linked their name to such a devastating disease. Once upon a time she and Dale would have sprawled on the couch together, watching the news, eating ice cream from the tub with two spoons, scoffing at the arrogance and ignorance of someone wanting to be remembered that way

Despite the rigours of cleansing every item and person who entered, it was peaceful once inside the inner buildings and offices of the House. Other than her own home, if she ignores the laundry and bathroom, there was nowhere else Kate feels she can relax and let down her guard. Here, within the rooms and halls carpeted with thick wool and the luxurious bathrooms and even the brightly lit staff cafeteria, she is confident in her safety; the Cabinet were all ensconced within the buildings, housed in hastily furnished temporary accommodation, and Kate knew their safety was guaranteed, and by default, her own. While she is here at work, at least.

She makes her way through the intertwined knot of hallways and rooms that only years of service and kilometres of pacing could prepare anyone for. Hapless interns routinely arrived at meetings late and flustered, stuttering apologies about having again taken a wrong turn.

Kate's heart has been fluttering in anticipation since stepping into the building, but now, as she nears her destination it is pounding in her chest, the hammering echoing into her stomach, and sending vibrations lower.

Lachlan is standing beside his antique desk, on the phone in his office when she arrives, but he looks up through the open doorway as she appears, and his slow smile and raised eyebrow rocket her heart rate skyward. She quickly looks away and busies herself chatting with the other staff milling around the outer

office they all share, their four desks now shoved together to accommodate a leather chesterfield lounge and heavy timber coffee table. The furniture has been moved from inside Senator Wolfe's office to make way for a double bed, small fridge, and array of personal items. He has been living in his office for many months now, using the en suite bathroom, working out in the Parliament gym, and eating in the Minister's lounge alongside the other members.
It is lunchtime before they are finally alone, taking advantage of fewer staff in the office to escape and with the door barely closed behind them Lachlan has her in his arms, kissing her deeply.

Kate melts. Kate always melts. Despite the guilt of knowing Dale is out there somewhere living through his very own horror show, despite knowing their daughters are nearby at the childcare centre, everything else evaporates except the heat of Lachlan's touch.

The affair is wrong, Kate knows that. Every part of her logical mind knows it. Every moral fibre within her silently screams obscenities in her mind whenever she is near Lachlan, but amidst the disaster that their lives had become, she feels powerless against the pull of him. It seems that in a world where death and terror and dark, dark sorrow beats at them all with unending relentlessness, Lachlan's touch, his hot breath on her throat, his powerful presence is the last thing to feel real. He makes her feel real. He makes her feel alive. He makes her *feel*, which was something Dale is unable to do.

The marriage she and Dale shares was good before the pandemic. Their once platonic friendship had blossomed into an easy love without effort or even a second thought. Despite sounding corny the cliché suited them because Dale truly *was* her best friend, and when he was not making her breathless with laughter, he was making sure she felt protected and secure. In the beginning they shared ridiculous jokes that made no sense to anyone else, and now they shared an entire life, two cheeky daughters and a mortgage large enough to be alarming.

From the time they met, more than ten years ago now, Dale had made Kate feel safe and it is the loss of that cocoon of sanctuary that Kate mourns most. At night, alone in the empty marital bed, when she is not draped naked across Lachlan's desk or mattress, Kate is racked with layer upon layer of guilt. The remorse is complex and complicated, and she struggles to atone for her cruel behaviour, even when faced with the knowledge she is not going to stop.

She often lies awake in the silence, hyper aware of Dale only metres away, uncomfortable on the camp cot and broken by all he has seen. Metres away in reality, yet when she reaches out for him with her heart he is too far away; he is unreachable to her. She lies awake, feeling like the worst kind of human, one who is blessed with the good fortune of a safe stable job and loving family, only to recklessly shit on it all like a spoiled child. She tosses and turns every night, the shame burning her skin, in a way that is not dissimilar to the heat that flushes her body on the nights she spends with Lachlan. She hates herself but that loathing faces outward to Dale whenever he comes home.

Hearing his footfall on the gravel that lines their driveway roils her stomach, as she imagines a waft of virus following him through the door into their home, like a wraith waiting to devour them all. Her panic has driven her to unreasonable requests, starting with the banishment of her husband to sleep alone in the laundry, where she leaves his meals, but from where she refuses to allow him to leave. Dale accepts every new rule, however unreasonable, because she knows — deep down - he wants nothing more than to keep them all safe. She knows how much he loves them all and how much he needs her support right now and yet she cannot reach out. At first it was the terror of contracting the illness that drew her back from Dale, or the fear of losing the children, but now her shame mixes and curdles with that corpulent dread and creates a toxic stew of confusion within her.

"We need to… We need to stop." Her voice stumbles over the words her head knows she must say, yet her body refuses to comply. Her skin goose bumps with pleasure as Lachlan's smooth palms travel up the bare skin of her back.

Lachlan's reply is a deep chuckle, muffled by her hair, as he nuzzles at her, ignoring her protests. "We don't," he says simply.

It has been like this for weeks now. Kate can sense Lachlan withdrawing emotionally and his refusal to discuss anything serious, anything about *them* and what they were doing is frustrating and confusing.

Before the lockdown, the pair had acknowledged the frisson of attraction between them, in the way colleagues sometimes could; their jokes were cheeky and their admiration of each other's skills was publicly commented on, without censure. Kate had been confident that the Senator found her interesting and listened to her because he valued her comments, not simply because he wanted to sleep with her. She had glowed in the warmth of his praise, but knew she was treated no differently to any other member of their team, and she had enjoyed similar easy, admiration filled relationships with other Members of Parliament and staff, as well as Lachlan.

That had all changed late one night when that fission burst into flames and engulfed them both in a furnace of passion that left her weak. With the girls quietly sleeping she had returned to the House, following yet another tense exchange with Dale about his work. On that night she knew she was being irrational, and she knew it was cruel to keep him away from them, but the thought of Dale touching her, or their sweet daughters, filled her with absurd anxiety, both then and now. Normally she refused to leave the house unless it was necessary and had not left the girls alone with their father since the outbreak, but the deep sorrow etched on Dale's kind face had forced her to flee.

In the early days of their affair she and Lachlan had spent as much time discovering each other's minds as they had exploring each other's bodies and the connection of sex and soul was intoxicating. As doubts pushed their way into Kate's psyche, she attempted to voice her fears, to seek Lachlan's support, to have him reveal himself to her again, but he silenced her with his mouth. As her body ached with a physical longing for him, her soul cried out for understanding.

Kate sometimes felt as much a victim of this illicit liaison as the clueless Dale, instead of the perpetrator, and the helplessness she feels creates an anger at being so weak, so blithely dismissive of her marriage.

Lately she has tried talking to Lachlan - who else was there?

"I feel like I'm letting everyone down by not being strong enough or moral enough to have avoided getting into this with you." No answer.

"Am I ruining all our lives?" No answer.

"It's not a 'happy' situation to be in at all you know, so I'm not 'having my cake and eating it' like people will think."

This last sentence is fiercely whispered across the desk and finally roused Lachlan to respond. He quickly glances at the door before tersely responding.

"No one will think that because no one will know." His face is closed as he spoke. Gone is the relaxed, tranquil expression he has shared with her over the last months. Gone is the gentle smile that turned her insides to molten liquid and chased all sense away.

Kate steps back at his words. His tone is bordering on brutal and the shocked look on her face brought that realisation to him. His brow softens and he steps from behind the paper laden oak table to move closer, but not before he shoots another look towards the open door and beyond it, the other staff.

"Sorry," he says. "Sorry, that came out wrong." He dares a brief touch, his long fingers resting lightly on hers, stiffly clenching a pile of cream-coloured files. "Can I see you tonight?"

Kate shakes her head. "Not tonight, but we need to talk. *I* need to talk about this." Not giving Lachlan a chance to reply she leaves the office and avoids him for the rest of the day.

She takes care to finish up her work before the others, knowing she cannot be the last to leave, and chance finding herself alone with her lover. She cringes internally. Lover is such a cheap, tawdry term. She cheerfully calls out a collective goodbye to the team, forcing light bravado into her voice, and choosing to include Lachlan in her airy farewell. She needs to get her head together and plan what she wants to say to him. What she wants to do with him. By rote she collects the girls and their still damp artwork from the on-site childcare centre and makes her way home through near empty streets, traffic delays a thing of the past. She always finished earlier than Dale (*unless she is busy acting immorally and with adulterous intent*, her tormented mind reminds her) so this evening she settles the kids in the loungeroom to play while she prepares the evening meal. For noise she clicks on the small flat screen TV flush mounted into the overhead cabinets by Dale, exactly as she had wanted. Her guilt painfully pokes her between the ribs again. She deliberately avoids the news channels, with their panic-inducing footage, and settles on a game show rerun. She pushes all thoughts of Dale and Lachlan from her mind and concentrates on winning the game from her kitchen.

When Dale arrives home later that night, she hears him enter the house, having shucked off outerwear and boots at the door, then the whoosh of the shower running full blast. From experience she knows he will undress in the cubicle with the water running then spend a long time scrubbing his body and clothing with the acrid smelling disinfectant soap that his department supplied. His clothing then went into the washer dryer with more soap and disinfectant; the hum of the machine provided the evening soundtrack to their new normal.

From the kitchen she hears Dale try to capture the girl's attention and draw them closer to the plastic curtain that formed an unnatural shield between them. Kate hears Bridie crawl across the house to where her father waited, chatter nonsensically for a few moments then return to the play mat. Taylor pays little attention at all, despite Dale's efforts.

Later when the house is silent and Kate is alone in the dark, wide bed, she unwillingly lets her emotions out from within the tightly clamped part of her consciousness and allows them to flood forward. Heavy tears flow down her cheeks where she lies, creating cool damp patches on the pillow, as guilt, sadness, shame, and regret create a cacophony of anguish. Kate cries for the woman she used to be, for the love she and Dale once shared and for the uncertainty of their futures. She sobs for those from whom the virus had robbed so much already, and for the world that would emerge after the crisis was over. She wails at the thought of the pandemic not ever being controlled, then again at the thought of losing her family. For the first time in so, so long Kate allows her fears a voice, and once permission is given the volume is overwhelming. Time passes as she wrestlers with the emotions as they collide and splinter until she is weak from the efforts and has no more tears to give.

Her consciousness returns to the house, only now it is not so quiet. From the direction of the laundry Kate can hear the melodies of a love song, their wedding song, playing just loudly enough for her to hear her through the empty rooms. The lyrics end, then immediately start again, from the opening notes; Dale has the song on repeat, just as he had done for her during both her labours, when the end stage pain had threatened to break her.

It is then that her heart knows. She slips from the bed and pads barefoot across the tiled floors until she stands in front of the plastic shower curtain, in place at the laundry door. In the lonely moonlit room Dale is seated on the edge of his cot, elbows on his knees and his head lowered into both hands. He is crying noiselessly.

Without thought Kate reaches up and pulls the curtain free of its thumbtacks. Startled from his melancholy Dale looks up, his eyes shining bright with tears, then disbelief.

Wordlessly Kate offers him her hand, which he takes after only a second's hesitation. She helps him to his feet, then leads him to their room, and their bed, where they hold each other in silent desperation.

Words are not needed; they have each other.

CHAPTER 6 - THE SENATOR

Lachlan hears Kate's casual, cheery departure from the outer office and notes the early hour, and his inclusion in the group farewell, and, with surprise, recognises their time together is over. The heaviness that has weighed down his heart over the past weeks grows substantially and delivers an unfamiliar sense of loss directly to the centre of his broad chest. The emotion makes Lachlan uncomfortable and he shifts his weight uneasily in the ergonomically designed desk chair.

When Lachlan was elected - as expected - he had met the team inherited from his predecessor with little initial interest. He expected a dry crowd of skilled professionals and a few of his staff were exactly this; very experienced in the nuances of the jungle that is the back rooms of the House, but also entrenched in their habits and customs. They were drab and so very uninteresting beige, but Lachlan did not criticise them for it; he knew they had seen many politicians come and go over the years and a certain measure of boarded fatigue was to be expected. God knows, over his own lifetime Lachlan had endured too many dinner parties with stodgy legislators, and understood the lethargy that came over one, when exposed to the tedious bastards for too long.

Then he had met Kate.

From the files and staff notes provided to him before his move to the city he knew Kate had been employed by the previous Senator as his personal assistant, and the simple fact she had been able to tolerate his crusty bigotry had created an image in Lachlan's mind of an insipid pushover. The instant they met the Senator knew this picture was far from the truth. On that day Kate had been dressed in all black, but the large jade earrings had reflected her emerald eyes and the jangle of similarly toned bangles had chimed musically up her slender arm when she confidently stepped forward to shake his hand. She was young, energetic, and outspoken, but her views were carefully considered and backed up by research and fact. Kate had been able to provide him with more insider knowledge of the workings of the House and the power plays simmering behind closed doors than any of his highly paid election experts, or even his own domineering father. Lachlan had quickly learned that to take his father's facts as truth was to miss the full story, and often that information was downright untrue, but with Kate at his side he was able to rapidly line up colleagues in order of usefulness.

Lachlan's road to the Senate was paved from birth, laid by his father, and encouraged by his mother. His parents were self-made and remarkably successful; from the family farm to a multi-faceted business Lewis Wolfe had grafted from before dawn till beyond dusk, ambitious and ruthless, and aggressively driven to rise to the very top of the market. Dawn Wolfe was similarly goal-oriented and wore the title of Trophy Wife with ironic ridicule - she worked just as hard as Lewis, polishing and re-defining the family's image towards the goal of perfection she and her husband shared. Together, the pair were unstoppable.

In his oldest sister they fostered her athletic prowess, bringing in acclaimed coaches and trainers from across the country even before she had finished school, determined to wring every ounce of potential from their first born. They were proud of her, of that

Lachlan had no doubt, but accomplishments in their family were always tempered with an expectation of further progress. Sara married well, delivered him two gorgeous nieces he unexpectedly and unreservedly adored, and now spent her time as an ex-Olympian promoting her husband's journalism career. Her path to supportive, powerful spouse had been similarly laid by their parents, and Lachlan sometimes despaired their mother would soon turn her attentions to her granddaughters and temper the wild impulsiveness he so whole-heartedly delighted in.

Throughout his life sport played a social role for Lachlan and while he can hold his own on the tennis court or cricket field, it is due more to well-coached technical skill than any real talent and it is not where his passion lies. He routinely loses out to Sara in any game they play which she enjoys immensely, and loudly.

For Lachlan, words and information are what drive him forward. From a young age he read his father's daily newspapers, devouring the information and pestering Lewis with questions, demanding explanations of the intricacies of the back stories to the news. He loved to debate and enjoyed the rush of power he experienced as he demolished an opponent with fact, wit and the ability to deliver an entrancing monologue. Politics seemed an obvious choice for him, according to his parents, and he was happy to agree. His university, his social group, even his girlfriends were all part of a larger plan to convey him to the House, and with scarcely any barriers the plan was successful. He realises now how few true obstacles he has ever faced, and how inadequately prepared he is to be part of the machine leading the country through the crisis that grips them. At least he is not alone - no one could have foreseen the devastation that has quickly become obscenely commonplace across the globe.

He enters his parents' home, nods a greeting to the reassuringly familiar sight of Marg, who is stirring simmering pots in the kitchen - his mother refuses to call Marg a maid, but she lives in the house, does all the cooking, co-ordinates the cleaning and gardening contractors and organises minor repairs to the sprawling three story home. Marg smiles warmly, and winks at him, then gestures towards the dining room.

He returns her wink with one of his own and moves through the house to find his parents.

Lewis is selecting a wine from the selection atop an antique buffet and his mother is sitting on the low sofa in front of a flickering open fire. Lachlan plants a brief kiss on her cheek and nods at his father before dropping into an armchair beside the fireplace.

"Lachlan!" Dawn admonishes "Don't sit so heavily, for heaven's sake. This is our home, not one of your pal's bachelor pads."

Lachlan pointedly looks at her outstretched legs and stockinged feet, tucked up neatly beside her on the lounge, her shoes discarded below her. "Comfy?" he asks, one eyebrow raised.

Dawn smiles, her unlined face softens, and she raises her own eyebrow, a skill only mother and son share, that infuriates Lewis and Sara. "Touché," she laughs.

Behind them Lewis clears his throat. "Merlot or scotch?" he enquires.

Drink selections made and delivered into the waiting hands of his wife and their heir, Lewis moves to stand in front of the fireplace and leans one elbow on the oak mantle. It is a stance Lachlan recognises; from childhood, through his youth and into adulthood, this posture meant only one thing - his parents have gathered him to talk.

"What is it, Dad?" Lachlan is weary and keen for whatever bad news or lecture Lewis must share to begin, so they can eat then he can return to the House and try to sleep.

Lewis does not bother with preamble, as is his nature. Over the decades many have found his approach abrupt and grating, but tonight Lachlan is ready to skip the small talk, to finally end this day.

"The PA. And you. It must end. It cannot continue." Lewis's sentences are short, his tone flat but his voice unwavering. The message is clear and delivered without emotion, like so many directives Lachlan has endured in the past. Lachlan swirls the scotch in the short glass, allowing the ice cubes to clink in the silence. He does not look up to Lewis, who has fallen quiet.

"Darling," Now it is his mother's turn, slipping into the role she plays in these family discussions, the one to soften the blows and smooth out any fuss. "It is such a strange time but when all this ..." she gestures vaguely with a manicured hand and struggles to find the words she seeks "... unpleasantness ends you need to be in a position to progress the migration bill as planned."

Confusion, Lachlan thinks. Only his mother, the unflappable Ms Wolfe would dismiss a pandemic as simply confusing, when so many other adjectives could be chosen. Horror. Dread. Sorrow. Hopelessness.

She pauses but when Lachlan remains quiet she lightens her voice further. "I am sure you agree the affair has no long-term future, but I have met Kate and she is a wonderful asset to you and quite an interesting woman, so I can see your," she pauses "attraction. But I agree with your father - there is no benefit to being caught in a gossipy neighbourhood drama between a staffer and her husband."

To hear Kate described in such a way is dreadful. No one knows her the way Lachlan does; no one else even sees her the way he does, but he knows discussing his heartbreak with these two is futile. He doubts that either of them ever allows emotion to reach their core or joy to electrify their souls, and for an instant he feels a twinge of pity for them both. He pushes that sympathy away as he downs the drink and rises from the armchair.

He moves towards the open doorway speaking carefully over his shoulder, to portray carelessness and alleviate the weight of the words.

"No need to worry. It is already over. Just a bit of entertainment while staying at the House, you know. Nothing serious and her husband has no idea." He leans through the doorway and motions to Marg, who takes his cue and brings in their meals, setting fine china in front of the three place settings. Marg will eat in the kitchen in front of a small TV and Lachlan wishes he could wind back the clock to his childhood and join her.

The conversation during the meal is all business. Lewis laments the lack of imported raw materials for his business, now that sea freight has halted, and descends into a bigotry filled rant about foreign students and the spread of the virus. Lachlan does not bother to correct him. Life is easier when Lewis believes everyone in his presence agrees with him.

Dawn and Lachlan talk soberly about who is ill and which funerals will be held in the coming days. As they discuss lifelong friends Dawn's eyes flicker toward her husband, almost 20 years her senior and Lachlan knows she worries about his complacency in the face of the pandemic. She and his CEO had turned the guest quarters on the other side of the pool into a home office, filled with all the technology required to monitor the empire in safety, but Lewis was too obstinate. His driver had taken to calling Dawn whenever he was summoned, and most of the time she was able to intervene and convince Lewis not to leave their sanctuary, but not always. His stubbornness was legendary.

The meal over, Lachlan escapes, ignoring Marg's home cooked desserts and his mother's sad eyes and returns to the House. The drive takes barely 20 minutes through empty streets and the whole time Lachlan struggles to keep Kate out of his mind. He is not successful. He already misses her smile, her throaty laugh that erupts when she is surprised and her kind, wise, creative mind. Intelligent women are rare in Lachlan's life. Beauty is available at every turn.

Alluring and exquisite women always competed for his attention, even now, but a woman with the raw confidence to challenge him? That quality belongs to Kate alone.

Lachlan did not expect their affair, although he can admit he enjoyed their subtle flirting and innuendo, and he knows if the world had not changed so disastrously, she would not ever have crossed that invisible line. He knows now - *had he always known?* - that their time together was wrong, but he had thought that perhaps when all this is over society would be different and they could be together in some way that was accepted. Many politicians survived scandals much larger than stealing someone else's wife. But Kate was not to be stolen.

Lachlan knows that her attempts to speak to him over the past weeks were an effort to progress their relationship and that his dismissiveness had become frustrating to her but in truth the thought of having that conversation terrified him. Lachlan laid claim to a charmed history of swooning young - and not so young - women who he had enjoyed passing the time with, in his bed, at social gatherings and, for a handful of marriage prospects, at family gatherings. Yet none had touched him; not as an equal, not as completely as Kate had.

Lachlan knows he is not a complete asshole when it came to affairs of the heart, and he remained close friends to many he had once shared passionate liaisons with, because it was not in his nature to be cruel. But he was determined and honest, and when a fling became tedious or unproductive, he simply moved on, after first explaining the ending in such a way that he remained a charming lothario, rather than a complete cad. For many women, and sometimes their mothers, Lachlan was the perfect man; the one who got away.

His flirtations with Kate began almost instinctively; it is his nature to disarm the women around him with his cheeky repartee and dazzling smile, while similarly enchanting the powerful men around him, with his success, legacy, and ambition. Kate and he shared saucy innuendos that became more brazen as their mutual respect grew, but Lachlan soon realised inside this gorgeous creature was a ball of energy and wisdom, he became more enthralled by her.

Lying on the hard, small bed, with its unfamiliar pillows and scratchy sheets, jostled into his office in the quiet House of Parliament, he allows himself to acknowledge the loss Kate's love would be. As his feelings for her grew, from pleasurable conquest to intellectual equal, his yearning for something deeper had both surprised and concerned him. Kate does not fit his plans; she is a married mother with two small children from a working-class background who works for him and none of this would remotely be considered acceptable. Lachlan smirks ruefully into the darkness and imagines how differently tonight's conversation could have gone, if only he could be honest to them all. He can imagine his mother's horrified face and accompanying gasps. His father would splutter at his disobedience in disbelief.

"No," he could have said. "I love her in a way I have never loved before. She makes me feel worthy and as if anything is possible, and I will not give her up. I will fight for her; fight with all that I am because she is worth it."

The uncharacteristic swell of emotions leaves Lachlan feeling breathless. His head spins with regret, loss, and confusion. How the hell did he allow this to happen? How the hell did he let her get under his skin? How the hell was he going to pretend none of it mattered in a few short hours, when he faced her across the table at morning briefing?

Restless and unable to quieten his overactive brain, Lachlan rises and angrily dresses in gym gear, before stomping through the dim, noiseless halls. The gym is empty, and he is grateful for the solitude. Glancing at the clock he calculates he has a couple of hours to exorcise Kate from his mind, vowing to strip emotion from his body with the punishment of sweat. With grim determination he finishes his warm-up and stabs at the control panel of the treadmill, upping the pace as music pounds inside his ear drums, delivered directly to his system by high tech headphones. With effort he drowns out all thought and concentrates on the beat, his feet and the force needed to bring his life back into a sense of familiar, albeit lonely, control.

CHAPTER 7 - THE GREY WOLFE

From the dining room Lewis Wolfe overhears Lachlan's warm farewell to Marg and feels an annoying prickle of envy at the easy relationship the two share, no matter how long they have been apart. He shakes the jealousy off as his son's footsteps fade, reminding himself of his role in Lachlan's life. As far as Lewis is concerned father and son are not destined to be friends; his job is - and always has been - is to raise the family's profile, stature, and bank balance. He is consoled by knowing his money is ultimately the one thing that keeps Marg loyal and available to Lachlan.

Hard work and long days have brought Lewis to today, to the position he holds, in this city and the country beyond. After years of cultivating careful friendship and business contacts, his single-minded determination to succeed left little time for dalliances with soft sentiments. He knows this portrays him as stern, cold, and unfeeling, but he also admits only to himself the thrill of feeling powerful and feared, as the formidable paragon of industry.

Sara delights Lewis: his daughter has enamoured him from a young age and they both knew it. He admires her competitive spirit and her understanding of strategy and was no prouder than when she willingly made sacrifices for success. Unfortunately, their close bond is just as obvious to Lachlan. More unsettlingly, it is obvious to Dawn, and Lewis has lived through four decades of pursed lips and his wife's incessant demands to include the boy.

Lewis admires Lachlan, surely Dawns knows this to be true, but their relationship was so much harder for Lewis. In his son he saw so much potential, and on the surface, Lewis begrudgingly admits, Lachlan's career has progressed well, but the boy - man - lacks the passion and the drive to ignite Lewis' interest for long. If he had been able to combine the best characteristics of both his children the family would be unstoppable, but when this admission was uttered during a marital argument many years ago Dawn had been shocked into horrified silence.

"For god's sake, Lewis." She had recovered her voice and raged at him. "You must see that we cannot push our children to the point we lose them! Surely even you can see that."

Even you, she had said. *Even you.* She had sneered those words at him, suddenly no longer the elegant, graceful woman he had married. In those words, spat at him in disgust, she had revealed how she truly felt about him. Her mask had slipped, just for a second, but in that moment, Lewis had felt their disconnection as if it was a physical wrenching.

Regardless of that night he admired Dawn, now, as ever. He knew her background, he knew how hard she had worked to pull herself up and away from her past, and when they had discussed marriage it was businesslike and earnest, but not entirely devoid of affection. They shared a hunger for wealth and prosperity, to secure the future for their children, and from that grew an esteem that eventually settled into a quiet, symbiotic love.

Passion was not for them. Lewis has experienced the madness of lust and infatuation a few times over the years, but even as those storms brewed, erupted, and then broke, he kept the objects of his attention far away from his home, his wife, his family and his life. He knows Dawn has her distractions, but they have not ever bothered him, and that is something he can say with confidence; he and Dawn are a formidable team that simply belongs together. A few years ago he believes Dawn had considered leaving him, as her romance with the American writer became serious, but without fanfare or even conversation the brash Yankee disappeared from their social circle, and their lives continued on as if nothing had occurred.

As he readies for sleep Lewis recalls the dismissive way Lachlan spoke of the staffer and hopes for all their sakes his son can recover and drag some truth into the words he had spoken to them.

CHAPTER 8 – DAWN'S REGRET

Dawn Wolfe has worked tirelessly to recreate herself. Australia is a country that tends to take people at face value, with few questions about heritage and lineage, and as long as Dawn continues to host the most sought-after fundraisers and campaign dinners, the questions about her past would remain unasked, and so, unanswered.

She knows the matrons of the city had suspicions early on, but the years of determined toil to cement her place at the top of society's metaphoric food chain, and the support given to Lewis as he bombarded the city with his success, had provided many alternate tales to appease the gossipers.

She also recognises, with a deeply felt gratitude, that Lewis has cushioned her entry into the city, and the small, yet powerful circle of people who run it. At barely 20 when they met, she had been naive but ambitious, and as her respect for Lewis grew, she saw the many, many advantages she would enjoy, as his wife.

To describe their marriage as businesslike was unkind however, and surprisingly far from the truth. Their marriage was not one that fairy tales would be based on, but instead their mutual appetite for power, their protectiveness of their children and their shared reliance on each other as kindred spirits had created something unique and precious. Dawn loved Lewis, a simple fact that sometimes - even now - startled her. Love had not been part of their deal, but over the shared years, respect had bloomed into care and affection, which matured into a deep love, around the time Sara was born.

To see Lewis, the powerful Mr Wolfe, soften into a gentle, quiet father, cradling their tiny child in his large capable hands has opened a part of Dawn's heart that had previously been closed to him, and with a rush of emotion that was unexpected love bloomed effortlessly.

Love was not something Dawn had ever expected for herself. Her mother showed her little, preferring the company of a parade of boyfriends that varied in appearance and kindness and seemed to cycle in and out of their lives every few years. Her childhood was spent in a series of Council flats, tiny, rented houses and, for a short time, her grandparents' home, but they are all just shadowy memories now. As soon as Dawn was able to work, she struck out on her own, living in a share house as she finished high school, scrimping and saving so she could follow the excitement and move into the heart of the city.

It was at the share house she met him and was instantly intoxicated by his presence. He was tall, with dark skin and hair that he wore too long, and when he turned his attention to her, she was entranced. He took her to smoke-filled bars where unknown bands banged out ferocious music, and small pockets of greenery where they picnicked like children. He spoke to her as an equal and invited her thoughts on every topic, hungry to know more and open her eyes to the world. He wove his magic across her heart and her body and when he disappeared as quickly as he had arrived, it was as if he had vanished into the fog that hung in the damp deep of a winter morning. The shock of his evaporation enveloped her in a deep depression; once again she had been tossed aside, discarded without thought, and she felt she was drowning in the loss. Dawn had moved mechanically for a long time, living by rote, only working and sleeping, until the fluttering in her stomach heralded an undeniable new truth. When the pain started and the time came, she gave birth alone, and when the infant, a plump, wriggling, baby boy, was taken from the room by a nurse, she dressed painfully and walked from the hospital.

The image of tiny fingernails and a sleeping face so achingly familiar has haunted her dreams across more than 35 years, but on that day, Dawn hardened her heart and vowed to change her own future; never again would she be abandoned and never again would she feel unworthy.

Arriving in the city, she took any job available but resolutely worked her way onto the reception desk of one of the best hotels, not the largest in the capital, but undoubtedly one of the best. She quickly learned that discretion was power and knowing some of the secrets of the powerful was intoxicating, and she watched the denizens with interest. She mimicked the softly commanding voices of the elegant women who sailed through the foyer, learning to round her vowels and fully pronounce every syllable. She noted the upright stature of the men who commanded the most respect from their peers and straightened her own spine in response. She built a simple wardrobe of well fitting, well-made clothes and learned how to stride in tall heels with enough sway to attract attention, without appearing immodest. It took an immense amount of willpower to avoid wondering about her son, the marvel of his hesitant first steps and the strangers who would celebrate his first words.

A regular guest at the hotel, Lewis appeared at her reception desk early one evening and without preamble invited her to join him for dinner. Dawn remembers feeling almost uneasy at the unexpected request, but curiosity overruled her disquiet, and later that evening she anxiously sat across a small linen covered table from a stranger. She had expected little more than an opportunity to practise her new persona, but Lewis was entertaining in a way she did not foresee, and the challenge of debating with this interesting man was surprisingly intoxicating.

From that night they met regularly, whenever Lewis had a free evening or lunch hour, and when he asked her to accompany him to the annual New Year's Eve ball at the Grand, she felt a shift in their relationship. For the first time she accepted his invitation to share his penthouse suite, and from there their shared fate was sealed.

To begin with Dawn was dismissed by Lewis' colleagues as a whimsy, a tasty piece on the side, even after their small wedding ceremony and honeymoon in Europe, but she strove until they changed their minds. She transformed his ugly, dark mansion into a stylish, light-filled home in which she held small intimate dinner parties and summer Sundays in the garden for the city's elite. That won over the wives and mistresses - she often hosted both, separately, of course - who were starved for any sort of entertainment and quickly they scrambled for a place on the invite lists.

It took longer to convince the men that she was a serious contender for their attention. She read ferociously and Lewis patiently taught her the subtleties of the deals he brokered. Slowly she became a respected conversationalist and - more importantly - recognised as her husband's ally, and she laid claim to a considerable amount of power.

Over the years she invested her own money and built an independent wealth and became a sought-after donor and patron to the multitude of needy charities that filled her email inbox with pleas for her time and money. She dabbled in charities that focussed on animal cruelty and preservation but mostly supported the organisations that mentored young women. She steered clear of orphanages; even those based overseas would have demanded photo shoots full of grateful cherubs, and that would be too much for that fragile part of her soul, the part she worked hard to protect.

Lewis knew all about the baby. Their marriage held no secrets. Oh, of course there were the dalliances they both amused themselves with, and while their mutual respect drew the line at sharing sordid details, each knew of various affairs, but they held true the knowledge of the solid foundation their marriage sat upon.

Before she accepted his offer of marriage Dawn told Lewis of her past, starting with her scattered, love-starved childhood, and ending with the long slow walk from the maternity hospital that led her to him. His response was kind; uncommitted yet considerate, and the wedding planning simply continued. Dawn assumes the next time - the only time - Lewis considered the abandoned child was the morning following Sara's birth, when her emotions spilled over and the tears from years ago rained down atop the newborn's fuzz covered head. Shocked, she had turned away, ashamed of the depth of this sorrow, but Lewis had gently coaxed her into his arms and held her and Sara tightly, the three of them rocking gently on the hospital bed.

The memory brings a sad smile to Dawn's face, and a fresh wave of worry that soon, too soon, one of her small, treasured family would be struck down by the virulent VS-202. Sara's home was conscientiously isolating, and the children were being home-schooled by an expensive French tutor, an imposing woman who was breezing them through their set work, while also teaching them the fundamentals of art and music. Lately Dawn found her taxing to be around, the woman's self-confidence had become dreadfully intimidating, but the children seemed to be thriving under her instruction. Lachlan was ensconced in the House, but who knew how well sanitation considerations were being managed, or the threat this PA brought in from the outside. At least he had agreed to end the liaison, and Dawn crossed her mental fingers that he spoke the truth.

The worry was more present than ever, not that Dawn would admit it to anyone. *I can hardly bear to admit it to myself,* she thinks. *But it is all too, too much.* Stifling an anxious sigh - sighing is such a ridiculously melodramatic female thing to do - she pulls the phone from her pocket and once again listens to the short message, allowing space for this new concern.

"It's Max, Mrs Wolfe. We have located him, Logan Pell. He's living in the eastern suburbs. I'll email you the full report as soon as I am back at the office, but it's safe to say we have found the target."

There is a pause, and on the recording, Dawn can hear Max rustling pages and imagines the private investigator is calling from inside his chaotic car slash office. "I just wanted you to know." His voice is suffused with a warm, benevolent triumph, at a job well done, and a cause well served.

She ends the call with a manicured fingertip that trembles slightly. The call came in while she was discussing menus and food shortages with Marg, but in the last few minutes she has listened to the memo several times, as if to confirm the reality of the information.

The investigator has worked swiftly, and to herself she admits a private pride in choosing such an efficient and discreet sleuth. She has used Max's services many times, in more business-related matters, yet when she video called him no more than six weeks ago, she had been quickly reassured that this most intimate of requests would be handled well.

"Mrs Wolfe," Max had said, his bland face - so perfect for his chosen profession - locked eyes with her, from one small screen to another. "I am sorry you have dealt with this alone. I will give it my full attention."

Dawn had been caught unawares by this unexpected kindness and marvelled at the capacity for people to show bright pockets of gentle understanding, despite the perilous state of the world right now. She had been forced to sign off the call abruptly, to gain control of the flood of emotion that swamped her.

The decision to find her son had surprised Dawn. For years, the thought of making contact was as alien as returning to the small, cramped ghetto suburb from which she had escaped, yet the uncertainty during this pandemic has awakened a yearning she cannot explain. I don't need to meet him. I just want to know he is alright, that I did the right thing.

She provided Max with the scant details she had; a date of birth, a copy of two crinkled newspaper articles, and the details of the Church organisation that took the infant in. From there, she had dared to dream that the former detective would fill in the hard to bear blanks, and today he had confirmed that confidence. Determined to occupy herself until the fated email arrives, Dawn quickly changes into a swimsuit and dives into the indoor pool, swimming lap after lap as the life-changing information downloads to her laptop upstairs.

CHAPTER 9 – FULL CIRCLE

Dawn steps from the large sedan and looks at the unassuming weatherboard house in front of her. The garden has two squares of weedy lawn, spliced by a cracked concrete path, that leads to a dirty brown front door, closed tightly against the world. She locks the car, more from habit than need, as the street is all but deserted, and slowly walks up the short path. Two shallow steps raise her onto an open porch, where a single wooden chair sits beside an abandoned beer can, that lives a second life as an ashtray. The home does not seem untidy, but gives off an air of disuse, as do many in the hushed neighbourhood.

Pushing back her shoulders to brace herself, Dawn knocks sharply on the wooden door, as her breath catches in her throat.

The journey from email to front porch is a blur to Dawn. She read Max's email as the salty drops from the pool dripped onto the thick carpet of her study, leaving a dry imprint of her bare feet. The only part of her that was dry were her trembling hands, hastily wiped on the thick towel Marg left beside the pool's edge whenever Dawn dived in. Acting automatically, she logged into her email and devoured the information, before showering and carefully dressing, styling her hair and applying make-up as armour against the emotions that raced within her.

She declined the offer of their driver to convey her, and reversed her personal car from the garage, following the directions of the robotic voice of the satellite guidance system through deserted streets, into the suburbs. She needed to make this sojourn alone.

She can hear no noise behind the door and as she strains to hear, her second knock seems to echo through the rooms inside. She refers to the printed page folded in her palm, confirming she was indeed at the address Max's investigation has provided.

Dawn feels the hammering in her heart rapidly slow, as disappointment drags the pace from its earlier excitement, and it instead thuds dully in her ears. She had not considered he - Logan - would not be here.

A wave of fatigue sweeps through her and Dawn stumbles with unusual unco-ordination, and she reaches out to the porch post to steady herself.

Perhaps he is an essential worker. Perhaps I just need to wait.

She settles into the creaking wooden chair, sits her designer handbag on the floorboards beside her and crosses her elegant hands in her lap.

I shall wait.

Next door Fairy and Tasmin debate furiously. The vehicle passing their own front window was odd enough to cause them to look up from the television, where they sat, watching an old Western, Fairy's favourite genre. Nowadays only those terrible white vans passed that house, so the sight of a car - an actual *car* - brought them both to the window. When it stopped out the front of her former home Tasmin had stiffened, as terror filled her body and caused adrenaline to spark in her fingers and toes.

Breathless, tears now fill her eyes as she pleads with Fairy.

"I've gotta go," she says, her eyes wild with fear. "Someone knows what I have done. Someone has come for me." She looks like a cornered animal, darting her eyes around the room, as if planning her escape, and Fairy's heart breaks for the girl all over again. *Would she ever heal?*

Ever the voice of reason, Fairy covers her own concern with bluff.

"Bullshit," she replies. "How could anyone know? Calm down, you ninny. Let's just see what happens."

They huddle together, whispering feverishly, as the woman knocks a second time, then sits in the same spot Logan once sat. Where he waited for Tasmin to return home from work, a lifetime ago, feeding his impatience with beer and cannabis. Where the questions began.

"Work late, did ya? Making extra, or making out with the boss?" The teasing enquiries always had an edge, but jokes became less amusing as their relationship descended into hell. It had been easier to resign and stay home, than face the endless accusations and backhands for back chatting.

"Oh God! She isn't leaving!" Tasmin's panic is filling the room, threatening to suffocate them both so Fairy leads her to the squat sofa and pushes her down into it.

"Stay here," the older woman says firmly. "I'll go see what she is doing. It might just be another charity worker, or perhaps someone checking up on you now that his body has been collected." The van had come for him two weeks ago; three weeks since the unlikely pair had become house mates, because Fairy has waited a full seven days to call in an anonymous death tip. *Seven days to make sure the prick is really dead.* Together they had watched from behind the lace curtain, as the plastic wrapped effigy was wheeled down that same path the unknown woman had just used.

Tasmin trembles mutely, but nods.

Dawn sees the woman as soon as she steps from the porch of the well-kept cottage beside her. The street is so eerily still that the movement instantly caught her attention, but Dawn had been hoping to see a man appear. A man named Logan Pell. Her son.

Instead, a short elderly woman with a wild mess of long grey hair appears at the edge of the verandah. "Hello," the old lady says. She keeps her distance. Dawn rises from the splintery seat, and with effort rearranges the disappointment on her face into a polite smile.

"Good afternoon," she says, striving to sound as pleasant as possible. "I am looking for Mr Pell. Logan." She gestures towards the house. "I believe he lives here."

"That's right," Fairy is deliberately noncommittal.

"Do you know where he is?" Dawn asks, unable to erase the hope from her voice.

"Why do you want to know?"

Dawn is irritated now. Who is this strange woman?

"Look," she says, her lips forming a combative pursed line. "It is important I speak with Mr Pell, so if you are able to assist, I would be grateful. Otherwise, I will simply wait." Dawn sat, as if to emphasise her point.

There is a pause while Fairy tries to get a grasp of the situation, and this elegant stranger with questions. Questions that could be dangerous.

Dawn waits, knowing the value of silence in any negotiation, but not knowing exactly why this conversation has become so weighty.

Curiouser and curiouser, she thinks.

Finally, the small woman speaks. "He won't be back," she nods towards the closed front door. "The bloke from this house. Logan. He's dead. The van came a few weeks ago."

Blood rushes into Dawn's ears, filling them with the sound of crashing waves, as disappointment and sorrow and regret collide in her heart. She is glad she is seated because right now she feels quite strange. Quiet faint. *How very odd*, she thinks. *I've never fainted in my life.*

"You alright?" Fairy's voice brings Dawn abruptly back from the brink of somewhere foreign, but her mind hovers, ever ready to make the leap into oblivion, to escape this dreadful, dreadful reality. The effect is an uncharacteristic helplessness that emanates from Dawn and causes her hands to shake as they rise to clasp at her breast.

"I'm... I'm..." she falters trying to focus on the tiny figure in front of her. From her vantage point on the porch Fairy appears extremely far away, and sort of blurry, almost soft around the edges.
I'm going mad.

"Come on," Fairy gestures to the shuddering woman. "Come with me. I'll make you a cuppa and you can tell me why you need to see Logan. Perhaps I can help," she adds, cryptically but Dawn is beyond comprehension. She rises wordlessly, descends the steps, and follows the woman across the matching patches of lawn. Keeping their distance is second nature and no further words are spoken until Dawn has cleaned her hands in the bucket of soapy disinfectant laden water on the porch that Fairy points to and donned a papery face mask. Fairy keeps a stash of masks on the table beside the front door, weighed down by a garish ceramic bullfrog, to keep them from blowing down the deserted street. Dawn does not hesitate and ties the mask behind her head before she steps carefully inside.

Tasmin has not moved and looks up with terrified eyes as the stranger enters the room, followed by Fairy.

"Go and make the cuppas," Fairy instructs tersely, knowing she now has two fractured women to keep calm, if she is to keep everyone safe, and the secrets secure.

Someone has to sort out these mental cases, or we're all in the shit house.

Tasmin scrambles to her feet and flees the room, which allows Fairy to lead the woman to the dining room, where she seats her at one end of the gleaming wooden table. Moving to the other end, Fairy prepares two chairs, one each for Tasmin and herself. When the frightened girl reappears, Fairy takes over, firing beverage related questions to the woman, who answers in a monotone.

Eventually they all have steaming mugs of strong coffee in front of them - Fairy detests tiny, overprice teacups, dismissing them as useless - and the conversation can be delayed no further.

"How do you know Logan," Dawn's voice quivers in a way she hates. *Get a bloody grip.*

Fairy can feel Tasmin's eyes dart to her but does not meet them.

"We've been neighbours for a few years," she answers, pleased that she sounds calmer than she feels. "How do you know him?"

Dawn raises her head. Hiding the truth did not matter now. Logan is dead and the pandemic has changed her world in such a way that an illegitimate child (*abandoned child*, her heart insists) would not so much as raise an eyebrow anymore. *And who cares if it does.*

The story tumbles from her, every aching detail of her life, then and now. Dawn speaks without pause until the coffee in front of her cools and leaves a ring on the inside of the mug, like a dirty high tide mark. Fairy and Tasmin listen without interruption and Fairy can feel the girl beside her relax and breathe more deeply, as imagined terrors disappear as Dawn's story comes to an end.

"So, you came here, I mean there, to meet him?" Tasmin's voice is quiet, but it does not waver, and Fairy is proudly relieved that she has bought her fear under control. *Atta girl.*

Dawn sighs heavily and then nods. "A few weeks too late," she says, tears filling her eyes and threatening to spill down her unlined cheek. Tasmin leaps to her feet, her natural instinct to hug the woman coming to the fore, but Fairy places a warning hand on her arm, and the girl hesitates. At first Dawn is confused, but as understanding reaches her, she quickly protests.

"Oh, it's ok." She scrabbles in her small handbag for the paper, and when she finds it, she waves it at them. "I'm clear. My family is tested weekly, because of my son's position."

My other son.

The paper is pushed from one end of the table to the other and Fairy picks it up to read, then narrows her eyes at the woman.

"Wolfe?" she asks. "As in Senator Wolfe? As in *the* Lewis Wolfe, the man who shut down the factory in Wentworth and put hundreds out of work?" Dawn is flustered now. "Well yes. I mean, I don't know about what happened to staff at the factory but yes. Lewis is my husband and Lachlan - Senator Wolfe - is my son." *My other son.*

She retrieves the health certificate and shoves it back into her purse. "I just wanted to let you know I am safe. You are safe." Her tone is defensive, and she juts her chin defiantly in Fairy's direction.

"I'm his wife," Tasmin speaks suddenly, and causes Fairy to jump. Jesus Christ, what is she thinking, silly sod? We almost had her out the damn door.

"His wife?" Dawn's confusion returns. "There was no mention of a wife in the report."

Fairy expertly arched an eyebrow. "Your Max also forgot to mention he was dead, too."

"Fairy! Please," Tasmin pleads, and for her sake Fairy makes the decision to retreat. She holds up both hands in rueful apology before she stands and collects up the trio of mugs.

"I'll put on a fresh brew."

Dawn's return journey flies, the car trip filled to overflowing with conflicting emotion and wrenching sadness. What a day this had been. Making the decision to find Logan had taken years, but in just a couple of months he had been found, only to be lost all over again, and in his place a timid, yet lovely young widow.

Dawn prides herself in being a good - no great, she decides - judge of character and Tasmin strikes her as a kind person, struggling no doubt, but lovely regardless. The two had agreed to stay in touch, despite the disapproval that sloughed from Tasmin's friend Fairy in undisguised waves. When she had paused on the front path to wave a shy goodbye at Tasmin, Dawn could not miss Fairy had hovering in the background, arms crossed tightly across her ample bosom.

That evening she fills Lewis in on the afternoon's adventure, omitting the derisive way Fairy spoke of him, of course. Not that Lewis would ever care what a faceless pensioner in the suburbs thought of his business decisions.

"Do you plan to see her again?" he enquires, sipping at his brandy, and watching her over the crystal snifter.

Dawn meets his gaze. "I do," she said simply.

"And Sara and Lachlan? What do you plan to tell them?"

She has thought about this too. "Nothing yet, but I will. When I know more, and when the time is right. They won't be able to get to know him, but once I know more about his childhood, and Tasmin is less fearful of us all, I would like to introduce them all." Lewis nods his agreement. Her answer has satisfied him, and his cautious but honest nature.

"Very well. Let's see what happens. Have you asked if she needs anything?"

Dawn smiles at him, her heart swelling with love for this incredible man. The corporate world saw only the driven, daring, ruthless side of her husband, and Dawn thinks how fortunate she was to be privy to this softer side. Practical, yet kind.

"Thank you, Lewis." Again, tears threaten and seeing them gleam Lewis covers her hand with his own across the embroidered tablecloth, purchased last time they had visited Paris. He pats her hand fondly, before rising and planting a gentle kiss on the top of her head.

"I'm going across to the office for a while. I have teleconferences for several hours, so don't wait up." With that, he is gone, and Dawn is left to rerun the day through her mind on an endless loop.

CHAPTER 10 – LOGAN PELL

Fairy enters the living room and is unexplainably irritated to see Dawn in her home again, cosying up to Tasmin, their phone screens alight, as they delightedly share stories and show each other the snapshots of their lives.

Dawn is now a regular visitor, arriving mid-morning on most days, and why not; nothing else filled their days as the lockdown stretched before them all, but her privilege meant travel restrictions bypassed the Wolfe empire. The Wolfe Corporation also arranged a weekly delivery of groceries, meaning the fortnightly trek to the nearest store was redundant. Now Tasmin and Fairy enjoy fresh vegetables and a much better quality of supplies than was possible from their local supermarket, which struggles endlessly to source fresh food. Soft bread, crunchy carrots and crisp lettuce grace their plates and every delivery also includes a gift for Tasmin - an exotically scented hand cream, a silk scarf or new, sought-after novel.

Tasmin blossomed. The food filled her belly and plumped her cheeks, and the haunted shadows in her eyes retreated further with each visit.

Fairy dreads the visits, and she is unable to feel anything other than distrust and vexation at each cheery knock on the front door. She swears - often openly and loudly - each time she hears the high-pitched, sign-song "Helloooo" from the porch, and only Tasmin's happiness stops her locking Miz Wolfe out.

Late at night Fairy attempts to unpack her grumpiness. It is jealousy? Is she envious of everything Dawn has, or is it resentment at being cast aside, when once it was she that provided solace and safety to young Tasmin? Either way, Dawn got under Fairy's weathered skin and gave her the powerful shits.

Having worked their way through the latest batch of happy snaps (*"Your nieces"* Dawn insisted on calling the two flaxen haired children captured in the small screen; Fairy despaired that if she rolled her eyes anymore, she'd have a stroke) Dawn gives Tasmin a more serious look.

"Do you know anything about Logan's childhood?" Her voice is quieter now, the subject more meaningful than updates about the grandchildren's French lessons.

Dawn had given full disclosure about Logan's conception and birth, including Fairy in the story, because the stubborn woman hung about their conversations like a petulant child. She irritates Dawn, who has decided to endure her for as long as Tasmin stays in this tiny home; Dawn's ultimate plan is for her daughter-in-law to move into the mansion, or at least the city apartment, where she could be kept safer until all this is over. She knows the old lady and Tasmin share a deep friendship, and does not want to act too soon, lest Fairy win that particular battle.

Tasmin pondered her answer before she said "I'm not sure how to tell you this Dawn, because I don't want to upset you, but Logan had an unhappy childhood. A really bad one." At seeing the shock cross Dawn's face, she rushes on. "It's not your fault. It isn't anyone's fault, it just wasn't, you know, good." She shrugs. "He didn't tell me a lot, but he has no family, because he was not ever adopted."

The families come and go, taking chosen children as if they are commodities. The babies and curly haired, pretty children are selected first, and over and over the unseen process of the draft passes him by.

Year after year he remains inside the system, finding little happiness in the grey world and enduring violence that bruises his thin body and hardens his young heart. Men in positions of power take advantage of his anonymity while the women in charge look the other way. His childhood is raped from him and he reacts the only way he knows how, by beating and tormenting the younger children with whom he shares the home.

At school he is behind before he begins, having none of the advantages of a loving home that his classmates blithely take for granted. No one at the home reads bedtime stories or helps him write his name, and as he progresses through the primary years he falls further and further behind. At high school his tough guy image is all he can call his own; his clothes, the food he eats, the bed he nightmares in, are all provided to him by the system, and those in charge remind him every day of the debt he incurs.

"When I met him, I thought he was so brave," Tasmin is crying now, and Dawn's horror incorrectly translates the tears as the grief of a soul mate, but Tasmin is mourning the girl she once was. Before Logan. Before his damage belted them both.

"He told me he had never celebrated a birthday, and the only way he knew he had turned 16 was because the authorities stopped looking for him when he ran away."

"Oh, my poor boy," Dawn is now sobbing, years of guilt erupting from her. "What did I do to you?" She looks from Tasmin to Fairy, pleading for understanding. "The paper said he had gone to the home but would be adopted!" She is nearing hysteria now. "They said he'd be adopted! Why wasn't he adopted? The babies are always adopted" The sobs wrack her body, and she crouches forward on the sofa, and wraps her arms around herself, to quell the torment raging through her.

"Apparently he was unwell as an infant," Fairy's voice from across the room is matter of fact. "Nothing terminal, but by the time he was in and out of hospital a few times he was past that cute stage, and no one wanted him." *Perhaps the ugly was already showing,* Fairy thinks.

Tasmin comforts Dawn and together they cry, so Fairy makes a swift exit to the kitchen. *More bloody cups of coffee she thinks ungraciously*, choosing to forget where the fancy coffee pod machine came from.

When she returns the pair on the sofa are more composed, but the detritus of the outburst is visible in the crumbled tissues and red-rimmed eyes.

"Here," she thrusts mugs towards the two, unceremoniously, before taking her own hot cup to the armchair furthest from the sofa.

Tasmin smiles gratefully. "Thanks Fairy. Where would I be without you?" The simple phrase fills the old woman with love, and not a small measure of triumph.

She takes a sip then speaks carefully, choosing her words. "Dawn has invited me to meet the rest of the family."

Fairy's head snaps up. "You've already met the old man, haven't you?" Tasmin nods.

"Yes. I have met Lewis, but I'd like to meet Lachlan and Sara and her children too." Her tone takes on a beseeching tone that instantly bristles the hairs on the nape of Fairy's neck.

She stares into the dark liquid in the mug, not looking at Tasmin, or the other women, as she says, "No business of mine."

"Would you like to come too?" By the way Dawn's face reacts it is obvious Tasmin has not discussed this with her host and Fairy is bolstered by that little fact. *Jesus it's hard keeping track of the points in this game*, she thinks, almost remorsefully. Almost, but not quite.

"No thank you very much," Fairy's response is full of bluster and dripping with overacting. "Into the city for dinner? Into the worst virus area? No thank you." Composure regained, she sits back into the easy chair.

Sensing a tiny victory Dawn rises and makes noises about getting home to arrange the dinner, planned for the very next evening. Her voice still cracks as she makes her farewells, but Fairy finds it hard to sympathise. *Be glad you DIDN'T know the bastard.*

When the quiet sedan draws up at the front of the home Fairy leaps from her vantage point in the front window and hurries to the kitchen where she busies herself stacking the dishwasher, a task she has deliberately left until now. When Tasmin appears in the doorway she feigns surprise.

"Hello love. Fancy a cuppa?" Fairy is determined not to ask about the evening spent at the home of the millionaire family.

"No thanks Fairy. But I do want to talk to you about something." Piqued Fairy follows her to the sofa where Tasmin shares Dawn's plan for her to move to the city.

"They are lovely people Fairy; I wish you had come too. If I move, I can study nursing and Sara said she has friends in the medical field who can tutor me." *I bet they aren't nurses though Tasmin, you naive nincompoop. They'll all be plastic surgeons and bloody brain surgeons and damn snobby dentists.*

"The city is still on very strict lockdown, but I'd be," she struggles for the right word, "insulated, I suppose, because everything is no contact delivery and order online. No one lines up for anything!" She is waiting for Fairy to react.

"What do you think?"

Fairy cannot speak for a heartbeat or two. Of course, she wants the best for Tasmin but how could anyone trust the genetics that contributed to the monster they had killed. There was that too - the murder.

"Do they know what he was like?" Fairy does not need to explain who she means.

Tasmin is taken aback. "Well, no. Not really. What difference would that make?"

"You thought he was worthwhile once and look how that turned out." The words are out of Fairy's mouth before she can stop them and the hurt that floods Tasmin's face makes her regret them instantly.

"I'm sorry love, but do you see what I mean? What if they're the same? All bright and shiny on the outside and complete arseholes once they have you?"

Tasmin speaks quietly. "I haven't decided anything, but I was hoping you'd be happy for me." She stands and leaves the room and Fairy hears the door to her bedroom close quietly.

"Fuck," Fairy says to the empty room around her.

Tasmin is in the shower when Dawn knocks on the door the next day, much earlier than usual, so Fairy lets her in.

After declining a drink Dawn asks if Tasmin had shared the success of the previous evening with her. *Success of the evening, Christ on a cracker I wish she'd lose the plum in her mouth.*

"Only that you want her to move in with you," Fairy replies flatly.

"You don't approve?"

"Why should I? She hardly knows you."

"She's family." Dawn's tone hardens.

Fairy snorts. "Only now because you've decided she is. Where were you when…" She stops abruptly, but Dawn urges her on.

"Don't hold back now. What do you mean where was I?"

Fairy looks at the woman in front of her, the epitome of all she detests, and snarls.

"He beat that poor girl to within an inch of her life. He smoked drugs and drank and beat her and went mad at the end, but it wasn't only the drugs that did it. He was always mad. A psychopath if you ask me." She points a gnarled finger at the air between them both. "He followed her wherever she went and made her quit her job and belted her till she passed out. He wasn't right in the head, if you ask me, and that poor girl, YOUR new family, nearly paid for it with her life."

"Fairy!" Tasmin's cry rang out across the room and bought a shocked end to the tirade. Fairy's chest heaves with the effort of her outburst and Dawn has paled visibly, but stands ramrod straight, refusing to show any of the tumult that fired within her.

"Is this true?" Dawn continues to face a huffing Fairy, but the question is obviously for Tasmin.

"Yes." The answer is given simply.

For a horrified moment Fairy thinks Dawn is going to vomit, but instead she turns and flees the house, the front door banging hard against the wall as she wrenches it open with force, such is her need to escape.

Dawn does not visit the next day, nor the day after that. The deliveries from the Wolfe Corporation continue uninterrupted but both Fairy and Tasmin are changed. Fairy is mortified at the damage she has done and filled with shame when she remembers the envy filled reason behind the dreadful words she spewed at Dawn. Tasmin quietly accepts her apology but her eyes have become dark again and the two move about each other as if they are strangers, merely sharing a house. Fairy believes the polite conversation is worse than if Tasmin had raged at her for what she has done. Instead, the happy girl has retreated, taking her back to the timid creature Fairy once rescued, one without a future nor dreams.

Fairy could not hate herself more.

CHAPTER 11 – THE SUNROOM

Dawn steadfastly ignores the trilling phone, and continues trawling through the list of email correspondence, expertly filing in order of importance. A week has passed since that dreadful day, when Fairy spewed forth the vile truth of her son, her damaged child, and the pain he had inflicted on Tasmin.

As soon as she had made her way back to the relative safety of her car and shut the door with a slam Dawn had called Max and, in faltering, broken statements, supplied him with the new, horrific information.

"I'm so sorry Mrs Wolfe," Max sounded mortified when they spoke. "The marriage is not registered anywhere, so was overlooked, but that is no excuse. I will start from scratch right now and be in touch."

His report arrived in her email inbox two days later, a dreadful list of Tasmin's injuries, those that were reported, Dawn admits, along with an inventory of disgruntled employers, several charges of assault arising from bar fights and road rage, resisting arrest and minor drug charges. Dawn read the screen with horror; all that Fairy had claimed was true, so appallingly true.

For the first time in many years Dawn had wearily closed the heavy drapes of her bedroom, took two sleeping pills, and collapsed into her bed, despite the mid-afternoon light.

The dreamless slumber did little. The next morning she awoke, feeling hungover and morose, her guilt gnawing away at her insides like an insidious rat. Her feelings were too complex to unravel, her shame and heartbreak too raw to untangle.

This is my fault, my responsibility. My actions, my sin, damaged an innocent child and when he fought back it was poor Tasmin that bore the brunt.

Dawn's regret is crippling, and as the phone rings again, Lewis ventures into her study, treading unusually carefully, as he comes to a stop at his wife's desk.

"Yes?" she says, her eyes not moving from the busy work on the screen.

"Are you intending to ignore that phone forever?"

"If I must." Her answer is curt, her posture rigid, so Lewis places a large hand gently on her shoulder as he speaks.

"You cannot blame yourself Dawn. You acted in the best interests of the child all those years ago and it is fate that intervened. Sometimes bad things happen, and our role is to move forward as best we can." He eyes the phone lying abandoned on the desk between them. "And you will not help anyone by ignoring the girl, or her blustering friend. You will not help them, and you are most certainly not helping yourself." He gives her shoulder one reassuring squeeze before he retreats.

Dawn closes the laptop with a snap and briefly leans her head against its cool surface. So many tears have been shed these past days, tears full of self-accusation and torment, and ignoring the girl so resolutely has drained all joy from her. Dawn is exhausted and has no idea of how she should feel or act or be, and so has chosen to hide instead. Her meals are taken either in the study or her bedroom, delivered by a thoughtful Marg, while Lewis has taken to sleeping in his office, allowing her the space he knows she needs.

Shaking Lewis' suggestions from her head she returns the focus to the work in front of her, a welcome distraction.

It is several hours later when a quiet tap at the study door rouses her and she calls out, startled, "Yes?"

The door cracks open and Marg's face appears around it. "Sorry to interrupt, but you have a visitor." Marg looks a little uncomfortable. "It's Miss Tasmin's friend, and Mr Wolfe has insisted she stay. They are having tea in the sunroom."

Dawn's face heats as the blood rushes to her head, but she nods stiffly.

"Very well," she says, dismissing Marg.

In the sunroom Fairy seems somehow even smaller, dwarfed by the enormous floor to ceiling windows that overlook rolling lawns and clipped hedges. She and Lewis are chatting amicably, and Dawn is peeved by the easy conversation that they are engaged in when she walks stiffly into the room and takes a seat.

"What do you want?" Her voice is flat.

Fairy has the grace to appear penitent, a quick flush staining her cheeks.

"I have come to apologise," her statement is simple. "I was delivering fact, no doubt, but I was unkind, and my motivation was uncharitable." Her words are unusually formal, illustrating a statement prepared well in advance, and her eyes now meet Dawn's and holds them steadily. "I am - was - oh hell, maybe still am - miffed at you coming in and taking Tasmin from me. Me! When it was me that patched her up and got her well again," Fairy's voice falters a little now, but she clears her throat and continues. "But I am bloody sorry for how I told you. And I am really bloody sorry for hurting Tasmin. She isn't well and she has stopped smiling and I wish to hell I could take it all back, and…"

Dawn cuts her off. "Tasmin isn't well? What do you mean, isn't well! It's not…" Her hand rises nervously to her throat, but Fairy quickly reassures Dawn, and Lewis, who has risen to stand beside his wife.

"It's not the virus! Oh God no, I wouldn't be here if it was," Fairy says as Dawn visibly relaxes. "She has some sort of stomach bug and is very run down." She pauses. "She misses you. That's a hard fact for me to swallow, but she does. Please don't turn your back on her now, just because of my big mouth. I've come here with my hat in my hands to ask you to visit her." With a grin she adds, "We have a flash new coffee machine that I'm sure you remember, but at the moment it's going to waste."

Lewis answers, causing both women to jump a little, such is their concentration on each other. "What a wonderful idea. Come Fairy, we shall drive you home now and you can try that machine out on me. I'd love to see Tasmin again."

The man sweeps them from the elegant home and seats himself in the passenger seat beside the stony-faced driver, leaving Dawn to share the soft leather back seat with Fairy.

"I'm so terribly ashamed." The admission is whispered as Dawn looks directly ahead, not daring to turn to face Fairy, as the car races through the street towards the little cottage. The old woman is uncommonly lost for words. *How the heck do I answer that?*

Unable to express her understanding any other way, Fairy simply reaches across and pats Dawn's hand, the gentle touch saying everything she cannot.

CHAPTER 12 – THE APARTMENT

Dawn watches Tasmin as she moves confidently around the small, modern kitchen preparing lunch for them both. She has once again lost the haunted look in her eyes and the worry lines on her forehead have been smoothed out by a cautious optimism.

It had taken patience and a united effort for Dawn and Fairy to convince the girl that moving to the apartment would be best, but gradually their arguments for the move had won her over.

Here she could be independent - for the first time in many, many years - yet she had both the protection of her new family and the support of Fairy, who checked in several times a day, by phone and even video call, when the connection was good. The video calls were a highlight; Fairy's grasp on technology was meagre but Tasmin suspects her bumbling calls, full of humorous glimpses of ears and ceiling are more for her entertainment, than a true indication of the old woman's ineptitude.

"Have you given any further thought to study?" Dawn keeps her tone light, fearful of appearing too involved, too controlling.

Tasmin has her back to her, as she prepares simple sandwiches on a benchtop filled with gleaming appliances. "Not yet," comes the reply.

Dawn wants to ask more but doesn't. I won't. I shall wait and just enjoy our visits.

The apartment has two airy bedrooms, a surprisingly spacious bathroom, the open plan kitchen and living room where they now sit, and a wide, sunny balcony on which Tasmin has started to grow vegetables. Lewis took control of the move, telling Dawn sternly that she needed to take a step back lest she overwhelm the girl, who still struggles daily to find her place in the world. Together Lewis and Tasmin had selected a range of furniture and fittings that gave the apartment a homely, yet uncluttered feel. The tones were classic; raw pine, crisp white and hints of navy and copper and in just a couple of weeks Tasmin had created a series of huge abstract canvases to hang on the empty walls. Dawn was quite impressed.

From her old home Tasmin brought only a few items. Fairy had accompanied her into the house next door, as the place still terrified her, and she retrieved some books and clothes, a tiny, knitted blanket and a couple of knickknacks. Among the pitiful haul was a tall wide-mouth mason jar, and inside that was a small, empty jam jar, its colourful metal lid screwed down tight. The jars now nestled between some tomato seedlings and a hairy fern out on the balcony, and it puzzled Dawn, but she did not ask. Dreadful things had happened in that house, and with Lewis' help, Dawn had come to see that she did not need to know the details of life - and death - at number 39. Instead, she and Tasmin, and even the ever-present Fairy, would only look to the future.

Tasmin places two lettuce filled sandwiches on the bench and perches beside Dawn on a wooden stool.

"About study," she says, filling with the sandwich with crunchy lettuce, and Dawn prepares for some disappointment. *Oh, why would she not let them help her? They wanted to help her!*

Tasmin turns her lovely face to Dawn, a face that Dawn realises is finally calm and secure. The girl has put on weight and the hard sorrow that clung to her has been softened and rounded by her newfound peace, and she is more beautiful than ever.

"Study is going to be postponed for a while. I'm having a baby." The words are few but the momentous meaning behind them instantly brings prickly tears to Dawn's eyes and she gasps instinctively.

"Oh Tasmin! Oh, I am so happy for you, for all of us. When are you due? Have you been well? Do you have a doctor?" The words tumble from her in an excited rush that would have Lewis groaning in exasperation if he were here.

Tasmin laughs, a tinkling sound that fills Dawn with joy. *I don't think I've ever heard her laugh.*

The girl takes her hand and looks squarely to Dawn. "I've known for a while. I suspected even before Logan…" she pauses "became sick, but at that time I didn't know if the baby would survive." Her voice becomes quiet. "I didn't know if I was going to make it some days."

The pain stabs at Dawn's heart and must reflect on her face because Tasmin quickly carries on.

"But I did. *We* did, and now you, and Lewis and Fairy and your family and I all have a baby to look forward to! I have seen the doctor once, and she thinks I am around 21 weeks along, but I am having an ultrasound on Thursday."

The tears are now spilling down Dawn's cheeks, but she does not care. A baby! Of all the rollercoasters of emotions over the past weeks seemed to pale into insignificance now there is a baby to fill them all with hope!

"I have asked Fairy to come with me to the ultrasound," *Ahhhh, that is why the loud Fairy is not with us for lunch today,* Dawn thinks, choosing to ignore the tiny, tiny pang of hurt that echoes, knowing Fairy knew this news first.

"I'd like you to come with me too. Please Dawn, if you can."

How she has changed. She is no longer a timid, broken child, no longer the bullied and battered wife. She is becoming the strong woman she was always meant to be, and this child will be raised by a loving parent in a sanctuary of a home.

"I would be honoured." Dawn cannot wait to tell Lewis and Sara and Lachy; a new baby to bolster the entire family, even if said child came with a grumpy Aunt Fairy in town. Family is what you make it.

Tasmin smiles warmly and bites into the sandwich, making exaggerated appreciative noises. "Ohhhhhhhhhh I love having fresh bread." The pair giggle - *I'm giggling for Christ's sake* - before Dawn can hold back no longer.

"What about a cot? And a pram? Will you want to paint the bedroom? I can get someone in, or Sara and I could come and help you - it'd be fun! …"

Krista Schade

EPILOGUE – BREAKING NEWS

"We interrupt your regular scheduling to bring you this breaking story.

"Scientists at Civil Laboratory have announced the Phase 3 human trials of the VS-202 vaccine have been successful and have released a statement acknowledging the Government support for the immediate release of the vaccine.

"The Office of Health Minister has also released a statement just now, which says they are working with states and territories on a release schedule and have allocated funding to the laboratory to fast-track production.

"The lab claims the vaccine has had no serious side effects, has shown to have a 94 percent effectiveness rate, and is administered via injection. It has been rumoured that scientists and medical teams have been working with Aboriginal Elders in the central deserts, raising questions about the use of bush medicines in this cure, but Civil Laboratories have not yet responded to these claims.

"Prime Minister Bonner has announced a joint press conference at 2pm today with the laboratory's chief scientist and representatives of the United Nations and World Health Organization, who have been overseeing the trial over the past weeks.

"The statement from the Civil Laboratory released just moments ago says that the vaccine is easily produced and in anticipation of the successful trial, more than 100,000 units are ready for distribution, and with Government support production would ramp up to producing double that number each week.

"Civil Laboratory made headlines early last month when they shared details of treatment trials with the Word Health Organisation and allowed access to the ground-breaking treatment regime to doctors in all affected countries, significantly raising survival rates.

"The regime includes a system of timed doses of Rodaxin, a readily available anti-viral medication, and high doses of vitamin C, extracts from the plasma of virus survivors and oxygen therapy.

"The availability of the successful medication combination has meant patients can quickly and easily commence treatment, avoiding the cardiac complications that claimed many lives at the start of the pandemic.

"Shareholders of Civil Laboratory voted overwhelmingly in a special motion, via video conference last month, to share the treatment, rather than market the breakthrough.

"Stay tuned as we cross live to the Prime Minister's address outside Parliament House in less than an hour, but it seems that our country could soon lead the world-wide recovery of the VS-202 pandemic."

Acknowledgments

Thank you to Liz and Kerri and all the other blog readers who received Tasmin and Fairy so enthusiastically that a short story became chapter one of this book.

Thank you to my wonderful mum Jo for reviewing and correcting my errors, alongside beta readers Kerri, Liz and Bert, and to Leanne for professional editorial advice.

Thank you to my husband and best friend Jas who fed me as I wrote and kept up the mugs of coffee as I edited.

I also owe a huge debt of gratitude to the online communities of writers at 20Booksto50k, The Writing Gals, Supporting Beginner Writers, and the Australian Writers' Centre; these forums have taught me so much.

155

 Krista Schade Writer

 kristaschadewriter